"Don't you want to sell me a house, Stephanie?"

"No. I'd just as soon pretend you weren't even here in town. And I don't know why you want me—" she broke off, fighting the waves of color that threatened to swamp her.

"I want you—" Jordan paused deliberately, running his eyes over her trim figure "—because I only deal with the best. And I'd rather have you working for me than against me."

"Well this time you are out of luck." Stephanie backed away from him. "Find yourself another agent."

Jordan smiled. "If you insist, my dear. Of course, I could tell your fiancé a few things about you. I'm sure you want to maintain the fiction that Katie is mine."

"Her name is Kathleen Anne Kendall," Stephanie said with bitter emphasis on the last word.

"Keep up that pretence and you might tempt me to go after my legal rights. What about it, Stephanie? Do we deal? Or—"

Leigh Michaels likes writing romance fiction spiced with humor and a dash of suspense and adventure. She holds a degree in journalism and teaches creative writing in Iowa. She and her husband, a photographer, have two children but include in their family a dog-pound mutt who thinks he's human and a Siamese "aristo-cat," both of whom have appeared in her books. When asked if her husband and children have also been characterized, the author pleads the Fifth Amendment.

Books by Leigh Michaels

Sell Me a Dream

Leigh Michaels

Harlequin Books

TORONTO • NEW YORK • LONDON
AMSTERDAM • PARIS • SYDNEY • HAMBURG
STOCKHOLM • ATHENS • TOKYO • MILAN

Original hardcover edition published in 1986
by Mills & Boon Limited

ISBN 0-373-02879-2

Harlequin Romance first edition December 1987
Second printing November 1987

For Barb and Tim Lemberger
so your friends will finally believe
that your mother really writes romances

CHAPTER ONE

THE wind had grown stronger, and brightly coloured leaves showered down from the thinning trees. Stephanie Kendall stood on the front steps of the sprawling new house and stared out across the rolling hills. She looked a little like an autumn leaf herself, with her auburn hair blowing in the cool breeze.

Behind her, a woman spoke. 'Stephanie, thank you,' she said, her voice a little breathless. 'I had to come out and look at it again, now that it's mine.' Her gesture took in the whole front of the house. 'It's always been my dream to own a house like this, and today it's become real. Thank you for helping me to find it.'

Stephanie smiled, and her face lit up. 'It was my pleasure, Mrs Bruce.' I don't make my living by selling houses, she thought, but by selling dreams. Real estate wasn't just a business to her. The joy of making dreams come true—of fanning the flicker of tentative interest in a house until it grew into a passionate love for four walls and a roof—that was the work of a good real estate agent. It was work that Stephanie loved.

Silly, she told herself. Selling houses is just another job. It was easy to be enthusiastic on the day a sale was closed, she thought, when the papers were signed, the cash handed over, the commissions paid. The rest of the time—the seemingly endless hours that she spent with Mrs Bruce and the dozens like her, inspecting every new listing—it was more difficult to be cheerful about the job of a real estate agent. But a day like today, and a sales commission the size of this one, made all the hours worthwhile. She could go home today with a clear head, knowing that she could pay her bills for the next few

months, until the next sale was finalised and the next
commission was paid.

'I'll send you an invitation to the housewarming!' Mrs
Bruce called, as Stephanie reached her car. 'You and
Tony both. I heard him say he was taking you out to
dinner tonight, so we won't keep him long over the rest
of the paperwork!'

Stephanie waved back. Then she manoeuvred her
little car down the winding drive and out on to the wide
street. It was one of the best neighbourhoods in town,
and one of the more expensive. And it was her first really
big sale. Until now, she'd handled the tract houses, the
bungalows, the ageing apartment buildings. But Tony,
the broker she worked for, had said that she was ready
for bigger things. With his help in the last few months
she'd sold several newer houses. Yes, she thought, the
career that had started off so quietly three years ago was
finally taking fire.

And there was Tony. She glanced down at the ring on
her left hand. The diamond set in the gold ring was
small, but it was good quality. Besides, Stephanie
thought, it was childish to want the flash and display of a
big diamond to show off. She was just as much engaged
with a small stone as with a full carat. Good, solid quality
would last.

The diamond in her ring was a little like Tony himself,
she thought. He wasn't handsome, and he was quite a
little older than Stephanie. But he was dependable, and
reliable, and honest—and those were the things that
mattered in the long run. Tony would never betray
her, never leave her, because she would be the most
important thing in his life.

The momentary vision of another man's face formed
in her mind, and she shook her head, trying to force it to
go away. But the image of dark hair and eyes the deep
blue of a tropical bay refused to leave her.

Why was she thinking of Jordan so much these last few

days, she wondered angrily. It had all been over long ago, when he had left her, and there was no reason to think about him any more. She would think about Tony instead.

She squashed the fleeting thought that Tony's reliability was hardly the stuff that passion was made of. 'I will never let myself be betrayed again,' she said firmly, and stopped the car in the driveway of her parents' house. 'And I will not think of Jordan any more.'

A thread of smoke rose from a pile of leaves near the kerb. Her father, standing near the pile with his rake, raised a hand in greeting. A tiny figure in a bright orange jacket extricated herself from another, deeper pile of leaves and came running to the car.

'Mommy!' she squealed in delight. 'Grampa's burnin' leaves, and Gramma's bakin' cookies, and—'

Stephanie picked up her squirming daughter and held her close. The child's rounded cheeks were pink with cold, and her big blue eyes were bright. Under the hood of her jacket, tendrils of dark hair peeked out . . .

And suddenly Stephanie realised why she thought of Jordan so often these days. For Katie was his daughter, too, and now that the chubbiness of babyhood was leaving her, she was growing to look more like him every day. The change had crept upon Stephanie so suddenly that the abrupt realisation was almost like finding a different child substituted for her own.

Why, Stephanie thought, why couldn't she have looked like me? It isn't fair that I must be reminded of him every time I see her—

No, she told herself. It isn't important who Katie looks like. No matter who her father was, she is my daughter now. That's the only thing that matters.

'Did you sell any dreams today?' Katie asked, practically.

Stephanie laughed. 'Yes, darling. One very large

dream, and we are—relatively speaking—rich. For the moment, at least.'

Katie looked puzzled. Then she wriggled out of Stephanie's arms. 'Does that mean I can have a bike now instead of that silly old tricycle?'

'Not quite. You're still a little young for that.' She swung Katie's hand high in hers as they crossed the lawn. Her father was putting out the fire, and billows of smoke rolled out of the pile of leaves.

'Not having much luck?' Stephanie asked.

Karl Daniels laughed. 'They're too wet—but burning leaves smell so good that I just had to try it anyway. I understand from the little news network there that Grandma is baking cookies.'

'If anyone would know, Katie would. She can smell chocolate chips from three blocks away.'

'I vote we go in and try a few,' he suggested.

The big kitchen was heavy with the aroma from the oven, and for a minute Stephanie thought she had walked back in time to the days of her own childhood. Coming in after school to the smell of bread or cookies or chocolate cake—if it wasn't for the child chattering beside her she could almost have forgotten the passage of years.

She kissed her mother's cheek and picked up a cookie fresh from the baking sheet. Anne Daniels smiled. 'You were always good at that trick,' she said.

'Dad taught me to always kiss the cook before I reached for a snack.'

Karl snorted. 'She's giving away all my secrets. Come on, Katie. Let's go clean up.'

As their voices died away down the hall, Stephanie draped her jacket over a chair and pulled up a stool. 'How was Katie today?'

'She's never any trouble, Stephanie. You know I love to have her around.'

'I know that you always say that. But I worry about

asking you to keep her, Mother. She's a handful for me, and I know that you—'

'Are you implying that I can't keep up with a four-year-old?' But Anne's voice was light. 'I'm happy to help out. I took her downtown today, by the way. Ingall's had a sale, and I found a lovely snowsuit for her. Now we just need boots and she'll be all ready for winter.'

'Mom—' Stephanie bit her tongue. They had had this argument a dozen times, and her mother always won. And, Stephanie had to admit, the financial help was hard to refuse. It took years in the real estate field before any kind of steady income was assured, and with Katie growing so fast it was hard to keep her clothed. But, at the same time, Stephanie's pride rebelled at the idea of anyone else being responsible for Katie. She had made that choice, had taken over that duty. It was her job, and hers alone, to be sure that her child was properly cared for . . .

And now that her father had been forced into early retirement when the company he worked for had closed, their budget was just as tight as Stephanie's own. Her mother didn't have the money to spend that she used to have, but she was still buying things for Katie. It made Stephanie uncomfortable.

'Did the closing go well today?' Anne asked. She took another tray of cookies from the oven.

'All according to plan. Mrs Bruce has her new house, and I'll get my commission cheque tomorrow, after Tony figures up his share.'

Anne sighed. 'It doesn't seem fair, does it, that you do all the work of selling a house and then he takes so much of it.'

'But he pays for all the office expenses, and for all the advertising, and for all the telephone calls.'

'I'd think that he'd work out a better deal with you than with the other salesmen he has. After all, Stephanie, you are a little different.'

Stephanie laughed. 'I may be engaged to him, but he is still running a business, after all, Mom. He has to turn a profit.' She bit into another cookie, and said indistinctly, 'He's taking me to dinner tonight to celebrate.'

'Will wonders never cease.' Anne bit her tongue, and then said, 'Sorry, that slipped out.'

Stephanie finished off her cookie, and asked curiously, 'Why don't you like Tony?'

Anne was silent a long time. Then she said, 'Where is he taking you for dinner?'

'You aren't going to answer my question, are you?'

'I wish you hadn't asked it.' Anne's eyes were troubled. 'If Tony is what you want, then Karl and I will welcome him into our family. But—'

'But you don't like the idea, do you? All I want to know is, why? What is it that you don't like about Tony?'

There was a long pause. 'Stephanie, I don't want to have resentments build up. It will be hard enough for you, starting out on a second marriage, without any tension between Tony and us.'

'I need an answer, Mom.'

For an instant, they were squared off, like boxers in a ring, as they had done in the days of Stephanie's teenage rebellions. Then Anne sighed, and said, 'I don't have anything against Tony, really. It's just a feeling. He's so darned inflexible, Stephanie. Every moment of his life is planned and detailed and mapped out.'

'He's very well organised,' Stephanie conceded.

'That's what I said. Inflexible. Nothing impromptu —nothing on the spur of the moment. He's obviously in no hurry to marry you—'

'I should think that would be a point in his favour!'

Anne seemed not to have heard the interruption. 'And he's always so darned neat. I'll bet he never went on a picnic in his life, because they're too messy.'

'Lots of people don't like picnics, Mom.'

'That's not the point, Stephanie, and you know

it. Children don't fit into moulds. I'm afraid for Katie—that he'll try to make her the perfect little girl, according to his rules—'

'Mother, he adores Katie. He's very willing to be her father.'

'But Katie already has a father, Stephanie.'

'Some father. He's never seen her, never shown any interest in her—' Or in me, she told herself, to soften the pang of conscience that gnawed at her. She had never told her mother the truth, that when Jordan had left he hadn't known about Katie. Then, irritably, she defended herself. She hadn't told him she was going to have a child because she hadn't known it herself. And he had never contacted her again, so there had been no chance to tell him. He didn't care—

Then, suspiciously, she asked, 'Why are you suddenly sticking up for Jordan, Mom?'

'I'm not,' Anne denied softly. 'I think what he did to you was dreadful. But Katie needs him, and you could stand the help. He should at least be sending you some money for her.'

'Mom, I don't need Jordan's help. Not his money—in case he has any—nor anything else. I'm earning my own way now. This commission today is the turning point. And as for Katie, she doesn't need Jordan, either. She'll be a lot better off with Tony as a stepfather than with the random support money that Jordan might be pushed into.'

'But he should be responsible—'

'I wouldn't bet that he'd take it seriously. Jordan was never wild about the idea of kids—I can't imagine that he'd worry himself about Katie just because I told him he should.'

Anne was shaking her head. 'He wouldn't feel that way if he once saw her. She's such a charming child, Stephanie—no father could turn his back on her.'

If you'd think about that, Mother, Stephanie thought,

you would know why I don't want to ask him for money.
I think you're wrong, but I'm taking no chances.

'And I think Jordan would do the right thing,' Anne
went on. 'After all, during the divorce, he offered you a
settlement—'

'Some settlement,' Stephanie muttered.

'I will never understand why you wouldn't take anything from him. You were proud, yes, but you should
have taken it for Katie if nothing else. It was a generous
offer—'

Stephanie sighed. 'To refresh your memory, Mother,
he offered me a percentage of his earnings. It sounded
generous, but, if you'll remember, he had left me for a
job in that rinky-dink outfit where they skipped paydays
altogether just to save the paperwork when the cheque
bounced. Jordan, the man who was going to set the
world on fire, was working for the fun of it.'

'But perhaps then you could have finished school,'
Anne said wistfully.

'Not quite, Mom. Twenty per cent of nothing is still
zero. It was an empty offer. He could have given me half
of everything he made, and I'd still have got zip, plus
a lot of aggravation in trying to collect. No, thanks. I'll
take care of myself—and Katie—without Jordan.'

Anne said tartly, 'It couldn't have been much more
uncertain than what you're doing now.'

'It takes time to get a start in real estate. But I'm there
now, Mom. If everyone will just be patient with me, with
Tony's help I can make it.'

'Accept his help. But please don't marry him, honey.'

'I'll marry whoever I want, Mom.'

'I know you will, dear.'

'Just what does that mean?' Stephanie asked suspiciously. 'You and Dad didn't want me to marry
Jordan, either—'

'That's right. We'd scarcely met him. And look what
happened!'

Stephanie counted to ten, and then she said, quietly, 'I'll try to forget that you said that. Now, I need to take Katie home so I can feed her and get ready to go out myself. Thanks for babysitting.'

Her mother said, 'I'm sorry, Stephanie, I shouldn't have said it.'

Stephanie paused in the doorway, her spine rigid. Then she walked on, as if she hadn't heard.

Her own little house looked snug and inviting under the spreading branches of the maple tree. Most of the leaves had dropped. 'That's our weekend project, Katie,' she told her as she released the buckle of the child's safety belt. 'Cleaning up the yard and getting it ready for winter.'

A wisp of smoke curled from the chimney. The day had grown steadily colder, and now the furnace was running. 'Tis the season for high utility bills, she thought, and then remembered the size of the cheque that Tony would be giving her tomorrow at the office. How she would have liked to have that money last winter! There had been so many things she had wanted to do in the house—to put a dishwasher in the kitchen, for one thing, and hang new curtains. Maybe put down carpeting in Katie's bedroom—the hardwood floors were so cold on small bare feet, and the child simply would not keep her shoes on.

But this year, with the house on the market, there was no point in investing in any of those things. She would sell it just as it was, and let the new owners dream of the improvements that she had planned for so long. Then she and Tony would use the money left over after the mortgage was paid as a down payment on a bigger house for all of them.

She was surprised that her mother hadn't asked if she had found a buyer for her house yet. But then, she thought, perhaps it wasn't unusual after all. Anne

Daniels probably didn't want to know the details; she probably included in her prayers every night a request that Stephanie's house would not sell, for she knew as well as anyone that, until it did, the wedding date would not be set.

Her mother was right about one thing, Stephanie admitted. Tony wasn't in any hurry to be married. Postponing the wedding had been his idea. Stephanie had wanted to go ahead with the ceremony and have Tony move into the little house. It would be cramped with all three of them, but it would only be for a little while, and they could save the rent he was paying on his apartment. But Tony had put his foot down. He would not, he said, be confined in a two-by-four house for the winter . . .

She paused on the porch as the teenager who lived next door came out with a rug to shake. 'Hi, Julie!' she called. 'Can you babysit tonight?'

'Sure. Where are you going?'

It was a friendly question, not a nosy one. Stephanie didn't hesitate. 'Tony's taking me to the country club for dinner.'

Julie grinned. 'Aren't we getting to be quite the social butterfly?' she laughed. 'Are you still going to speak to us little people, after you marry him and start going out to dinner every night?'

Stephanie laughed, but it was hollow. Tony belonged to the country club because he considered it necessary for someone in his position, but in all the time that she had worked for him, he had taken her there to dinner just a couple of times.

She was thinking about that as she started Katie's supper, explaining to herself that Tony was, like all good real estate people, simply careful with his spending in order to stretch his income over the low periods.

How different it had been in her first marriage, she thought. With both of them in school, money had been hard to come by, but when they had a windfall they had enjoyed every penny until it was gone—

And I am thinking about Jordan again, Stephanie realised, and told herself firmly to stop it.

Katie came into the kitchen. Her blue eyes focused on the single hamburger broiling in the oven, and she said flatly, 'I don't want Julie tonight.'

'Oh?' Stephanie looked down with mild interest at the small figure, hands defiantly planted on tiny hipbones, in the middle of the floor. 'Is this something personal against Julie, or are you objecting to babysitters in general?'

'I'm not a baby,' Katie said, with dignity.

'Pardon me. I'd forgotten that you're four now.'

'And I don't want Julie! I want you.' Katie's bottom lip was pushed out.

'That's a lovely pout, dear. You're doing it very well,' Stephanie applauded. 'As a matter of fact, you will have me all day tomorrow.'

'All day?' Katie asked suspiciously.

'That's right. I'm taking the day off to reward myself for today.'

Katie's big blue eyes summed up her victim. 'Tonight, too?'

'No. I am going out tonight.'

'I don't want you to go.'

'That's very flattering, love. Now, are you ready for supper?'

Katie looked thoughtful for a moment, as though she might begin a hunger strike and refuse nourishment altogether. Then she climbed up on her chair. 'I'm not hungry,' she announced.

'I'm not surprised, after Grandma's cookies.' Stephanie brewed herself a cup of tea and sat down across from Katie, who was arranging her green beans in a perfect line.

'Are you going out with Tony again?' Katie asked.

'Yes.'

'To sell dreams?'

Stephanie almost regretted sharing that phrase with Katie. 'No, dear. To have dinner.'

'I don't like Tony.'

For a moment, the stubborn line of Katie's jaw, the firm set of her eyes, was so like Jordan's that Stephanie thought she was seeing a ghost. 'Kathleen Kendall, you are suffering from an attack of the wicked green monster,' she told Katie.

Stephanie hadn't dated many men; her schedule was too unpredictable and Katie too much of a responsibility for most men to stay interested very long. But Tony was different. He was the first man who had kept coming back, and Katie had reacted firmly, badly, and predictably.

It was Stephanie's own fault, she told herself. She had spoiled Katie—she had been the child's world for too long. But Katie would get over it. She would grow to love Tony, as soon as they became a real family. Once she had a full-time father, she would quickly adjust.

Just as, she told herself, Katie always fussed when Stephanie went out for an evening and told her that she didn't want Julie to babysit. But once Julie was in the house and Stephanie was ready to leave, Katie would be perfectly agreeable. Unless, of course, Tony was there. In that case, Katie was capable of throwing a tantrum that could rock the whole west end of town . . .

'Monster?' Katie asked. Her blue eyes had got even larger.

Stephanie wished that she had put a closer guard on her tongue. 'Nothing, darling. I was only thinking aloud. What would you like to do tomorrow?'

Katie was still considering her answer when Julie knocked on the back door. 'Sorry I'm late, Stephanie,' she said, shedding a dripping cagoule.

'I hadn't even noticed that you were. When did it start raining?'

'Just a few minutes ago. It's coming down in buckets, though.' Julie ruffled Katie's hair and pulled out a chair at the table. 'I'll sit with her while she finishes eating,' she offered. 'Go get dressed. A glamorous date deserves a little special attention!'

Actually, it took very little time. Stephanie's wardrobe didn't run to glamorous; most of the things in her cupboard had been selected to coordinate with the dark blue blazer that was the standard uniform in Tony's office. The apple-green dress she put on had been a birthday gift from her mother the year before, but it still fitted perfectly. It brought out the green flecks in her hazel eyes and accented the auburn waves of her hair. She was putting on her wristwatch when she came out of her bedroom, and she stood in the centre of the living room, struggling with the catch, as she gave Julie her instructions.

'Katie doesn't have preschool tomorrow, so she can stay up a little later than usual. Mother sent home made cookies for a snack—'

Julie nodded. 'Chocolate chip, I hope,' she said. 'She makes the best ones in town. You forgot your earrings.'

Stephanie's hand went to her earlobe. 'Can't do that.'

Katie looked up from her building blocks. 'Let me pick,' she demanded.

'Very well. But hurry—' Katie wasn't listening. She had danced ahead into Stephanie's bedroom, and her small fingers were already exploring her mother's jewellery box by the time Stephanie caught up.

The child took her time, considering each earring, her tongue caught thoughtfully between her teeth. Then she picked up a set and put them into Stephanie's hand. 'These!' she said.

Stephanie looked thoughtfully at the delicate gold trinkets in her hand. Katie had good taste, she reflected.

She had chosen one of the few pairs of good earrings that Stephanie owned; most of her stock had come from the sale rack.

Julie had come in, too. 'I've never seen you wear those,' she said. 'They're pretty, Stephanie.'

Stephanie's fingertip stroked the delicate filigree, and then she deliberately fastened the hook through her earlobe. She couldn't remember the last time she had worn the earrings. They held too many memories, because they had been a gift from Jordan in one of the rare times when they had had money.

But it was silly to leave them hidden away in a drawer, she told herself. They were the prettiest things she owned, and it was time to put the memories away.

Memories, she thought, as she looked down at Katie, absorbed in exploring the tiny compartments of the jewellery case. I'm too young to have so much of my life tied up in memories.

The doorbell rang, and she went out to greet Tony with a smile.

CHAPTER TWO

TONY trimmed the last fragment of steak from the bone and speared it with satisfaction. 'These special cuts aren't bad, you know,' he said, 'though ordinarily I prefer a New York strip, since it doesn't have the bone. There's less waste that way.'

Then why didn't you order the steak you wanted? The question trembled on Stephanie's tongue, but she didn't ask it. She knew the answer, anyway—the T-bone dinner had been on special offer tonight, and the New York strip had not. It had saved Tony two dollars on the final bill.

She looked out of the big window that overlooked the pool house. Their table was tucked off in a corner, in an alcove away from the main dining room, and it was so quiet that they might almost have had the entire place to themselves. How Katie would love the club, she thought. As soon as they were married, Stephanie could bring her here. Katie could swim all year round here, and when she was a little older there would be tennis and golf lessons. It was a wonderful world for a child to grow up in.

'Have you heard any rumours about the McDonald plants going up for sale?' Tony asked.

Stephanie shook her head. 'Not a word. Why?'

Tony sounded worried. 'I talked to Jake McDonald last night, but I couldn't get anything out of him. I'd sure like to get that listing. Do you suppose your father would know anything about it? He used to work for McDonald, didn't he?'

You know perfectly well he did, Stephanie thought resentfully. You know that he took early retirement

21

when Jake McDonald's corporation went bankrupt, and
that since then he's been miserable and Mom has had to
be careful with their budget . . . But she bit her tongue
again. 'Dad didn't say anything about it, though I
scarcely had a chance to talk to him this afternoon.'

'He might not know, though,' Tony fussed. 'He was
only on the manufacturing line, after all. He wasn't in
the front office.'

'But he was a supervisor,' Stephanie reminded him.
'And Jake McDonald still calls him now and then.'

'I'd sure like to get that listing,' Tony said again.

'I hate to puncture your balloon, but who would you
sell it to? I can't think of anyone around here who wants
to buy a building big enough to manufacture aeroplanes
in. If Jake McDonald was smart, he'd call in a company
that specialises in industrial real estate.'

'Are you saying that I couldn't sell it?' Tony was
bristling.

'Not necessarily. It's just that your prospects are
limited, and it isn't a very saleable property anyway. It
will probably be sitting there empty for the next fifteen
years, no matter who tries to sell it.'

'But just think of it. The commission on that sale,
invested properly, would produce a nice income for
years, Stephanie.'

'Right.' There was no point in arguing with him, so she
changed the subject. 'I looked at the Evans house
yesterday.'

'The gorgeous Queen Anne on Maple Hill?'

'The one with the shingle cladding and the octagonal
room. Yes. They're very reasonable with the price,
too.'

'Do you have any prospects in mind?'

'A couple of them.' She took a deep breath. 'I think it
would be great for us, Tony.'

He looked horrified. 'That big barn?'

'A minute ago you called it—'

'That was before you went crazy on me. Think of the upkeep and utility costs on a big house like that.'

'I'm thinking of the space, Tony. That whole gorgeous third floor for a playroom for Katie, and the high ceilings, and all that luscious woodwork in the whole house—'

'You can't be serious, Stephanie. That house has at least five bedrooms.'

'Six, as a matter of fact. But I'd want one for a sewing room, and another to put the washer and dryer in so I don't have to carry laundry up and down stairs—'

'It has an open stairway, too, doesn't it?'

'Oak,' Stephanie said succinctly.

Tony shook his head. 'Those things are death on utility bills. Now if you'd put a couple of apartments on the second floor and at least one on the third floor—'

'That means we'd be cramped together worse than we would be in the house I have now.'

'Nevertheless, that's the only way we could afford to live there.'

She sighed unhappily. She knew in her heart that he was right. There was more than the purchase price of a house to be considered. The Evans house was nearly a hundred years old, built in the days before heating costs had soared out of sight. Living there would be prohibitively expensive, and it would get no cheaper as the years went on. 'Maybe we can build our own home,' she suggested.

Tony shook his head. 'I've seen too many people start out with a set amount of money to build a house, and by the time they're finished it costs twice that. And I can't see you staying inside a budget, Stephanie.'

He said it with a smile, but the words stung. *I've lived on a tighter budget than you for the last four years,* she felt like saying. But she didn't.

'As long as we're talking about houses,' Tony added, 'Beth Anderson stopped at the office this afternoon. She listed their house for sale and left a key. I want you to go look at it tomorrow.'

'But I'm taking the day off, Tony.' Then she realised that the name was a familiar one. 'Don't I know the Andersons? They have that big new house on West Elm, don't they?'

'That's right. It's a nice house—family room, a couple of fireplaces, big kitchen, office in the basement. Good location. Look it over and see what you think.'

She felt better. Perhaps Tony was looking for a house for them just as hard as she was, after all. The Anderson house sounds as if it could be just right for us, Stephanie thought. Katie would have so much space, and I could stop walking around toys in the living room all of the time. And we could work at home sometimes, too.

'I'll go over tomorrow,' she said.

'Good. She'll be at work, of course. Here's the key.' He pulled it out of his pocket.

Stephanie tucked it away in her handbag. 'Why are they selling?' she asked curiously. 'They built that house, and it's only a few years old—'

Tony shrugged. 'They're in a financial squeeze—like everyone else. That reminds me—'

Stephanie reached eagerly for the folded slip of paper that he held out. 'Thanks, Tony. I didn't expect you to stay late at the office to figure it out, though.'

'I thought you might like to have it tonight.' He discovered that his coffee cup was empty and started to look around for the waitress.

Stephanie glanced at the figures, and then held the cheque up so she could study it more closely. 'Tony,' she said finally, trying to keep her voice steady, 'I expected quite a little more than this. What happened? This cheque is a thousand dollars short of what I had figured.'

'I know. I put it in the company savings plan for you.'

'You did what?' She was horrified. 'I need that money now, Tony!'

'And you might need it more next year. You can't rely on a sale like the Bruce house every month, you know, Stephanie. Or even every year. You have to build a nest egg—'

'First I have to build a nest,' she said tartly. 'I had plans for that thousand dollars, Tony.'

'Necessary things, or frivolous ones?' He shook his head sadly. 'Stephanie, you have to learn that no one will plan ahead for you. You must do that.'

But I want to live now, too, she thought. I want a new dress, and I want to buy Katie that doll that she wants, and I want to have lunch out at least once a week instead of always running home to fix a sandwich. And I want to have a little money put away for fun things—a weekend trip next spring, perhaps. Is that asking for so much?

Then she sighed. Tony had been in the business a lot longer than she had, and he knew how easily a thousand dollars could slip through his fingers.

But is it so wrong of me, she thought rebelliously, to want to eat lobster now and then instead of tuna? Not every day, of course, but once in a while I need something special!

Once, she had planned to have a life that included lobster every night, if she chose. Her father had worked for years on the manufacturing line at the McDonald plant, and though he had always been well-paid, there had never been the fantastic clothes and trips and luxuries that Stephanie had dreamed of. And so, when she had begun to look around for career opportunities for herself, she had chosen a profession in which she could earn top money, as the mathematics expert who figured life and death tables for the insurance companies. She'd been half-way towards her goal when she had met Jordan, and suddenly nothing had seemed as important as he was.

The quick wedding in the college chapel, the fun of fixing up their first apartment, with imagination and hard work making up for lack of money, the joy of a girl's first passionate love affair—

And then her whole life had gone to pieces, she reflected, and the career dreams had gone down the drain along with her education and her marriage, and she had come home, a deserted wife, to have her baby alone.

Perhaps her mother was right after all, she thought. Jordan ought to be made to pay for what he had done to her.

'Since the waitress is apparently not going to get me another cup of coffee,' Tony grumbled, 'are you ready to go?'

And here I sit, Stephanie thought, at a table with my fiancé, thinking about my ex-husband for the hundredth time today. What in heaven's name is the matter with me?

Tony counted out a precise dollar in change for a tip. 'I wouldn't leave that much if it wasn't expected,' he growled. 'Maybe you'll make coffee?'

'Of course, if you like.' Stephanie laid her napkin aside and pushed her chair back.

The adjoining dining room was almost empty. Tony put his arm around her shoulders, and she looked up with a smile. In the far corner, three men were just rising from their table. One of them was joking with the waitress. Stephanie consulted her mental *Who's Who* and remembered him. He was the president of the local Chamber of Commerce, and the last time she had seen him was the day several months ago when he and his wife had signed the papers on the house she'd sold them. She sent him a pleasant smile.

One of the men with him looked up. 'Why, if it isn't little Stephanie. I haven't seen you in months, my dear.'

'Hello, Mr McDonald.' She offered her hand. She had always liked this man, her father's friend. He was gruff, but he had always been kind to her. She thought sometimes that he wished that his own daughter had been more like Stephanie, instead of taking after her social-climbing mother . . .

Beside her, Tony tensed, and she could almost feel the mental acrobatics he was going through. If the Chamber president and the owner of the biggest empty plant in town were having a jovial dinner with a stranger—then who was the stranger?

Stephanie's eyes focused on the back of the man's neck, where a white shirt collar met dark hair that lay perfectly along a well-shaped head . . .

Her heart was pounding so loudly that she was certain it was shaking the room. It can't be, she thought. It's only your bloody imagination, Stephanie—you've conjured him up from nothing.

Then he turned and, for Stephanie, time slowed to a crawl. The lights in the room seemed to dim, and somewhere, off to the side, someone began to speak. The voice sounded hollow and disembodied, and each syllable seemed to drag out for full minutes. The only thing that was real to Stephanie was the blue ice of Jordan Kendall's eyes.

She didn't know how long they stood there, but finally Jordan looked away from her and held his hand out to Tony. But it must not have been more than a split second, for no one seemed to notice anything strange about her.

'Here's the girl you need to talk to, Jordan,' the Chamber president was saying. 'She sold my wife our house, and Martha loves it. She'll find what you want. Stephanie, this is Jordan Kendall—he just bought McDonald's factory and now he needs a house. Jordan, Stephanie Kendall—' He broke off abruptly. 'Darned funny that you have the same last name,' he joked. 'That must make it a partnership made in heaven, right?'

Stephanie forced a laugh. 'Not funny at all, I'm afraid,' she said. 'We've—met before.'

Jordan's icy blue eyes were firmly set on her again. 'I seem to remember that you asked the judge for your maiden name to be returned as soon as our divorce was final.'

The Chamber president started to choke, and McDonald hit him on the back.

'It wasn't convenient,' Stephanie returned coolly. 'In the end, I preferred to keep your name after all. There are several good real estate people in town, Jordan. I hope you find one you can work with. Good night.' Her glance took in all the men, and she turned, spine straight, to walk across the big room, half expecting a steak knife to strike the middle of her back at any moment.

Jordan had looked as if he could do murder, she thought, with a shiver.

She was waiting by the door, huddled into her rain-coat, her hands deep in the pockets, when Tony came out of the dining room. 'My God, Stephanie, you look as if you've seen a ghost,' he snapped.

'And so I have. A very large, very solid, very angry ghost—' Why is he angry? she wondered, with half of her mind. Surely that should have all been over years ago; and after all, it was Jordan who had left her, not the other way round . . .

'The point is, you aren't married to him any more, and he wants to do business with you.'

'Where did you get that idea?'

'He told McDonald after you walked out that he might give you a call.' He ushered her into the front seat of his car and slammed the door.

'He was merely being polite,' Stephanie said stiffly as he slid behind the wheel. 'He wouldn't come to me if he wanted to buy a doghouse!'

'I can't believe that you turned him down! A man with money enough to buy McDonald's factory, and you refuse to sell him a house? Do you know what executive homes are selling for these days? And how few people can afford them?'

'Don't jump to conclusions. One can buy a factory without cold cash, you know—or at least without one's own cash. And who says he wants an executive house? Maybe he's not an executive—'

Tony shook his head. 'I never saw a blue-collar worker wearing a suit like that before.'

'And maybe he doesn't need a big house. After all, it's only him—'

'How do you know?'

Stephanie stopped dead in the middle of her tirade. Jordan—married? Jordan—with a family? 'No,' she said.

Tony shrugged. 'If we'd found a house we liked, you'd be married by now. What's preventing him from doing the same?'

'Jordan didn't like being married, that's what. It tied him down too much. He likes to make his own decisions.' Her voice was bitter, she knew. That, after all, was what had ended their marriage—Jordan's determination to decide for himself, without stopping to consider what she had wanted.

'It's no big deal, Stephanie. So you were married to him. This is a little town, and you're going to run into him. You'd better hash it out with yourself now and get over it.'

That much was true, she realised. It was too small a city for her to avoid him, even if he was also trying to stay away from her. With the purchase of the factory that had been the town's largest employer, he would automatically join the small group of leading citizens. Because of her job, they would move in similar circles.

Stephanie got her door key out of her handbag as Tony pulled into the driveway. 'Do you still want coffee?' she asked, hoping that he would say no.

She needed some time to think, she told herself. It had

been shock enough just to see him again, after so many years. But to adjust to the idea of Jordan Kendall living in the same town—that would take some time.

'Sure,' Tony said, as if surprised that she had asked.

The rain was pounding down again, and in the few steps from car to house Stephanie's raincoat was soaked through. Julie was waiting at the door. 'I heard the car, so I plugged the coffee pot in,' she said.

'You're an angel,' Stephanie told her. 'How was Katie?'

'Irritable. She wanted to wait for you before she went to bed, but she finally settled down. She was sleeping a minute ago.'

'Good.' The last thing I need to cope with tonight is Katie, she thought.

She stood by the door and watched till Julie was safely home. By the time she had turned the porch light off, Tony was coming back into the living room with his coffee. 'Did you want a cup?' he asked, almost as an afterthought.

She put her head back against the couch cushions. 'No, thanks.'

He sat down beside her and put his feet up with a sigh. 'Closing a sale is always so darned much work,' he said. 'And up till the moment that the last signature is dry, it can fall apart. It's no wonder so many brokers have ulcers.'

Stephanie had closed her eyes. She let the words flow over her, hardly hearing, wondering if that awful scene in the club had been only a nightmare. After so many years, for Jordan to turn up here—in this little town—It was scarcely believable.

'You still look pale,' Tony observed. 'Come on, Stephanie, it's not the end of the world. Nothing has changed, after all.'

But everything has changed, she thought, and remembered her mother's words that afternoon. Once Jordan sees Katie, he can't turn his back on her, Anne had said.

'Honey—' He put his arm around her and kissed her, a little awkwardly. 'It's all right.'

There was a thump from the next room. 'What was that?' Tony asked.

'Katie, I imagine.' Stephanie didn't move, but she did open her eyes. A minute later Katie appeared in the doorway, dark hair tousled, her thumb in her mouth, dragging a rag doll by the foot. She was wearing her favourite pyjamas, the bright yellow ones with the ducks printed on them. She had worn them nearly to death, and the bottoms were sagging, Stephanie noticed.

'I can't go to sleep,' Katie announced. Those all-seeing blue eyes snapped as she saw Tony's arm around her mother, and she crossed the room to crawl into Stephanie's lap.

'What's the problem?' Stephanie asked.

'The wicked green monster will 'tack me.'

'That's a new one,' Tony muttered.

'The wicked—What wicked green monster, Katie?'

'You told me.' Katie's voice was uncompromising, and her eyes as she looked at Tony were just as icy as Jordan's had been.

Stephanie let her memory run back over the day's conversations, and found the wicked green monster. She had been thinking about how jealous Katie was of Tony, and the expression had slipped out. 'How very appropriate your choice was, dear,' she said. 'There is no wicked green monster in your room.'

'But you said—'

'I was wrong. There is no monster at all, Katie, so it is perfectly safe for you to go to sleep.'

Katie turned that one over in her mind, and said, 'Can I sleep with you tonight?'

'Oh, for Pete's sake,' Tony muttered.

'No, dear,' Stephanie told her. 'But you may leave your door open and turn your nightlight on.'

'I'll take you back to bed, Katie,' Tony offered.

Katie summed him up with unblinking eyes. 'I don't want you. I want Mommy,' she announced.

'Mommy's tired,' he said.

'Then you go home,' Katie told him, with irrefutable logic.

'As a matter of fact,' Stephanie began.

'I guess I can't argue with both of you,' he said, and forced a smile. 'See you tomorrow, Stephanie.'

She walked to the door with him.

'She doesn't like me, does she?' Tony asked, darting a look over his shoulder at Katie.

'Nonsense. She just isn't used to sharing me with anyone. She'll be all right.'

'When?' Tony asked drily. 'By the time she graduates from college?'

Stephanie had no answer for that. She watched as his car disappeared down the rain-soaked street.

'I'm glad he's gone,' Katie announced when Stephanie took her back to her room. She climbed into her bed and heaved a mighty yawn. Within two minutes, she was asleep. The wicked green monster had not been mentioned again.

Stephanie turned out the lights and sat silent in the darkened living room.

So Jordan Kendall had come to this little city. Of all the towns in the nation, he had chosen this one. And quite obviously he intended to stay.

She wondered what he planned to build in the factory he now owned. She wondered where the money had come from to buy it. Was it his own, or was he working for someone else?

Five years had made little difference in him. He was better dressed now; Tony was not the only one who had recognised the hand of a master tailor. His hair was cut a little shorter, as if he paid more attention these days to grooming. But he was still the same Jordan that she remembered, in every other way.

He had always been uncommunicative, but she had felt tonight as if she had run into a brick wall. It was the way she had felt in the final days of their marriage. What happened to you, she wanted to scream at him. What made you cold and hard and distant?

There was some comfort in knowing that he had been as surprised and as shocked as she. In the years that had gone by, he had no doubt forgotten where Stephanie had grown up. Their few months together had been spent in the city; he'd never even visited this little town. Now, five years later, here they both were, horrified to find themselves thrown together, and unable to escape it.

It looked, at any rate, as if Jordan had succeeded in making something of himself, she thought idly. She was glad for him, but she wondered if he counted it worth the price—the sacrifice of their marriage.

For a moment she was back in the tiny bedroom of their apartment, the only home they had shared. She was facing a coldly furious Jordan again, and trying to explain—as she had been trying in vain, for weeks —why she would not quit school to follow him to some God-forsaken little town where a dreamer every bit as idealistic as Jordan himself had offered him a job. What he had not offered was any assurance that the job would last, that the pay would be enough for them to live on, that there would be any future. They would be pinning their faith on a vague chance, and Jordan would not try to understand that Stephanie—with her desire for security—was incapable of taking such a risk.

The discussion had turned to accusations, to screams, to tears—and then to agonised silence as Jordan had packed his belongings.

There hadn't been many of them. Jordan travelled light, and most of the things in the apartment were Stephanie's.

'Funny,' she mused. She hadn't noticed, at the time,

that in those few months of marriage he had brought home nothing of any size. A few clothes, a few trinkets —her hand went to the delicate earring—but nothing big. It was almost as if he had known he would not be staying long . . .

She had cried herself into oblivion after he left. When, two weeks later, there had still been no word, she had gathered her courage, called a lawyer, and started the long process of divorce.

She straightened up the living room, putting Katie's toys into a pile in the corner. Just the memory of Jordan's cold anger the night their marriage had splintered sent chills up her spine.

She had never talked to him again, until tonight. The cold civilities they had exchanged at the club would be the epitaph for their marriage. It would be easier next time they met, she told herself, and eventually there would be no pain at all, nothing left but the vague memories of a few months shared.

And Katie. She had forgotten for a moment about Katie. Sooner or later, someone would slip up and tell him about Katie.

'Damn you, Jordan Kendall,' she said, staring out at the rain. The thunder mimicked her internal war. 'After all these years, why did you have to come back and mess up my life now?'

CHAPTER THREE

STEPHANIE woke to a tuneless, repetitive little song from the foot of her bed. Katie saw her open her eyes and bounded up to greet her. 'Good morning, Mommy!'

Oh, for just a little of the cheerfulness of childhood, Stephanie groaned inwardly. 'It's my day off, Katie,' she moaned and buried her head in the pillow.

'Let's go to the store, OK? I'm hungry.'

Stephanie gave up and crawled out of bed. The blankets were all askew, she saw. She must have had an even more restless night than she had thought; she had awakened several times and lay there in the dark, frightened of the unknown monsters that threatened her peaceful life.

But now, in the morning light, it didn't look so awful. Even when Jordan found out about Katie, as he must sooner or later, it would make no difference. After all, Stephanie was asking nothing from him. And as for her mother's ideas that no father could turn his back on a sweet child like Katie—well, Anne Daniels had always been a romantic. Jordan had never shown an attraction to children, and no matter how charming Katie could be, she couldn't melt that six-foot-two block of ice. Which was just as well, Stephanie thought.

She stood in the shower for as long as she dared, letting the needles of hot water pound her troubles away. By the time she got out Katie had dressed herself and was wandering around waiting for zippers, buttons and shoelaces to be fastened. 'I'm hungry,' she repeated.

Stephanie was making a mental list of all the errands that had to be done. Stop at the Andersons' house as Tony had requested, deposit her commission cheque at the bank, grocery shop—'The heck with it, Katie,' she said. 'Let's go out for breakfast today.' It was a rare treat, and she supposed that she shouldn't spend the money when she could cook the same meal at home for pennies. Katie never ate more than a few bites anyway, no matter how much she protested that she was starving.

But Stephanie was still feeling rebellious about Tony withholding part of her commission to put in his enforced savings plan. He might be able to do that, but he couldn't tell her how to spend the rest of her money, she vowed.

She was sipping her coffee, and Katie was waiting impatiently for her bacon and eggs, when a group of men came into the coffee shop. Katie looked up with delight in her face and scrambled down from her chair to run to greet her grandfather.

Karl Daniels brought her back over to the table. 'It's a surprise to see you here, Stephanie,' he said. 'May I join you?'

'Of course. But we wouldn't be hurt if you sat with your friends.'

'Frankly,' he said, with a conspiratorial wink, 'I'm beginning to worry that being seen with them every morning is ruining my reputation. But I haven't had breakfast with two such lovely ladies in a long time.'

'For that kind of compliment, I'll even buy,' Stephanie offered. 'I'm rich today.'

'The commission cheque came through? I've eaten, thanks. But I'll have a cup of coffee.' He pulled out a chair.

The waitress brought their food just then, and Katie, surprisingly enough, tucked into her bacon and eggs as if she hadn't eaten in a week. Stephanie buttered her blueberry muffin and said, 'Do you have coffee with the guys every morning, Dad?'

'Just about. I get tired of sitting around the house.' He

laughed a little. 'And frankly, I think your mother is getting a little tired of me, too.'

'How do you feel about retirement now?' she asked softly.

'It was the only option I had at the time. But I'm bored, Stephanie.' There was no humour left in his voice. 'Damn bored.' Then he looked a little sheepish. 'All the things I always wanted to get done—now I don't want to do any of them. I have done all the pottering around the house I want to do in the next year, and raking leaves only takes one afternoon. I never was the kind for stamp collecting or that sort of nonsense, and—'

'You miss the people at work,' Stephanie deduced.

'That's about it,' he admitted. 'When you've supervised a dozen people's work for years, Steph, it's a big change to have only yourself to look out for.'

She held her cup up for a refill. 'Have you talked to Jake McDonald lately?'

'No. Why?'

'He sold the plant.'

'Really? What are the new owners going to do with it?' The gleam in his eyes made her regret that she had raised his hopes.

'I don't know. I just found out last night that it had been sold.' She raised her eyes from the dark brew in her cup, and said, her voice steady, 'Jordan is the one who bought it.'

'Jordan?' Karl's jaw tightened. 'What's he doing in this town, the lousy son of a—'

'Please don't, Dad,' she begged softly, darting a look at Katie. To her relief, the child was paying more attention to the grape jam on her toast than to the conversation. 'He was my husband, after all.'

'Some husband,' Karl said stiffly. 'He deserted you, left you stranded with a baby to raise, without a penny to help you out—'

'In the first place, Dad,' she said, regretting that she

had brought it up at all, 'Jordan didn't have a penny to give me. And if he had, I wouldn't have wanted it.'

'So where is the money coming from to buy McDonald's factory?'

'I don't know. He's probably acting for someone else. And——' Her tongue stuck on the admission she knew she should make. She should just come out and tell her father the truth. She should say. And he didn't know about the baby, either, Dad. But she couldn't force herself to form the words.

She reached across the table for his hand. 'Please, Dad, promise me that you won't do anything crazy,' she begged. 'I only told you because the sale is bound to be announced soon, and I didn't want it to surprise you.'

'Why here?' Karl muttered. 'Why did he have to come here?'

'I don't know. But I'm the one who has to deal with this. Please don't get yourself involved.'

The muscles in his arm were tense under her hand.

'Daddy, going after Jordan with a horsewhip isn't going to solve anything,' she pointed out. 'Especially for Katie and me.'

Katie looked up, as if puzzled by how she had got into the conversation.

Finally Karl relaxed. 'I don't have to like it,' he warned Stephanie. 'And if he does anything——'

'He won't, believe me,' she said. 'He was just as shocked last night as I was. He obviously wasn't expecting to see me here——'

'You saw him?'

'He was having dinner with Jake McDonald last night.'

A muscle twitched in his jaw. 'And he had the nerve to stand there and talk to you?'

'It wasn't a matter of nerve. The alternative was to create a very large scene in the middle of the country club.' Stephanie was beginning to see a flicker of humour in the situation now.

Her father didn't seem impressed. 'I'll warn your mother,' he said. 'And speaking of her—she told me about the squabble you two had yesterday.'

'It wasn't really a squabble, Dad.'

'At any rate, she's very sorry she said those things about Tony.'

Stephanie shrugged. 'She's entitled to say what she thinks. She has her opinion about Tony, and I have mine.'

'Tony's done very well for himself since he came to town,' Karl mused. 'But there's still something about the man I don't like any more than your mother does. Nevertheless, he's reliable, and that's a lot.'

'Yes,' Stephanie agreed, remembering how unreliable Jordan was. The waitress came back with the coffee pot, and Stephanie glanced at her watch. 'Heavens, I must get busy,' she said. 'Katie, we have to go look at a house this morning.'

'New listing?' her father asked.

'Yes. But Tony seems to think we might want to buy it.'

'Isn't that illegal, for an agent to buy a house for himself?'

'Not as long as the owner knows all the details.'

'Seems to me it's a little shady.' He had picked up his cup and was on his way to join his companions at their long table.

'Dad, surely you don't think Tony would do anything unethical?'

He snapped his fingers. 'Maybe that's it,' he said. 'I don't trust anyone who claims to be so damned straight!'

And that was a joke, Stephanie thought as she and Katie drove across town, for Karl Daniels was so straightforward himself that he was practically transparent.

The Anderson house was just as pretty as she had remembered it, nestled into the hollow of a hill. Its cedar cladding had weathered to an even silvery grey.

Stephanie had never been inside, and she cautioned Katie as she used her key.

She cautioned herself as well. Don't get your hopes up too far, she told herself. Every house she had liked, Tony had not. But he seemed to really like this one, so if she liked it too—

They wandered from room to room, soaking up the atmosphere of the house. Beth Anderson had tucked fresh flowers here and there, and scented candles left a fresh fragrance in the air. The rooms were neat, each cushion plumped up and in place. Stephanie fell in love with the kitchen, lined with oak cabinets and gleaming ceramic tile. There was a big room off to the side of the house, perfect for Katie's toys and Stephanie's sewing machine. The two bedrooms upstairs had quaint sloped ceilings, windows on three sides, huge wardrobes, and adjoining bathrooms.

Stephanie looked around the smaller bedroom, at the elegant wallpaper with its tiny print of pink flowers, and then glanced down at Katie, who was abnormally quiet beside her. 'How would you like to have this as your new bedroom?' she asked.

Katie looked around, and then shook her head definitely.

'But it's a nice room!'

'I like my other room.' It was firm.

Stephanie didn't argue. There would be time enough for convincing Katie when the sale was closed and they were ready to move. This room was twice as big as what Katie had now, she estimated. She would quickly learn to like the new house.

Stephanie locked the house up again and buckled Katie into the car. 'You know that we'll be moving to a new house soon,' she reminded Katie. 'It might even be that one.'

'I want our old house.'

Stephanie sighed but didn't pursue it. It must seem an

enormous change to Katie, for the little house was the only home she could remember. It was understandable that she rebelled against the idea of moving, and there was no sense in pushing her. Besides, Stephanie thought, when the child saw her own furniture in the new room, she would quickly adjust.

The Anderson house would be just about perfect, Stephanie thought. There would be plenty of space for the three of them, and even for another child, if they decided to expand their family. She'd talk to Tony first thing on Monday, as soon as she got to the office. No, she decided, on second thought. She'd call him when she got home. They might as well not wait another day.

She felt a prickle of sympathy for the Andersons. They must be having a bad financial crunch. Selling that gorgeous house would be a last resort.

She stopped the car and got out to move Katie's tricycle out of the drive. 'Kathleen,' she warned as she put the car in the garage, 'that is not a good place to leave your toys.'

'I'm sorry, Mommy.'

'Don't do it again. I'm going to start raking leaves and trimming the bushes for winter.'

'Can I help?'

Katie's definition of help left a little to be desired, but Stephanie nodded anyway, knowing how important it was that the child feel needed. 'You can start by looking for your little rake and shovel. I think you left them in the back yard last weekend.'

Katie wrinkled her nose and trailed off to find her child-sized tools. Stephanie checked on her a few minutes later to find that, tools forgotten, she had joined the little boy next door on his garden swing. Stephanie smiled and went back to work.

The pile of leaves had been steadily growing for an hour when a silver-coloured car came down the street, braked sharply, and pulled into her driveway. It was a late model, low-slung Lincoln with out-of-state plates, and it didn't take a genius to recognise Jordan behind the wheel.

Stephanie froze. Her first instinct was to call to Katie, to tell the child to hide. 'That would be a bit counter-productive,' she muttered to herself and put her rake down. She didn't know what he wanted, but she was going to get rid of him just as soon as she could.

Jordan was looking at her cosy little house, his dark eyebrows raised quizzically. As Stephanie approached, he turned that brooding gaze on her and said, 'Not the sort of neighbourhood I would have expected to find you in. Weren't you the one who wanted the high-level condo, preferably in New York City?'

'People change, Jordan.' She kept her voice cool, deliberate.

'Apparently they do,' he agreed quietly. 'You were the mathematics wizard of the university, but you're selling real estate in a little town instead of calculating life expectancies for a large insurance company. What happened, Stephanie?'

'My plans were—interrupted.'

He sounded mildly surprised. 'Oh? You led me to believe that you would let nothing get in your way.'

I didn't plan on a baby, Stephanie thought. There was enough money to feed myself and Katie, or to pay my tuition, but not for both, and so I came home.

'Selling real estate,' he mused. 'It seems a chancy sort of job for a woman who wanted financial security above everything else.'

Stephanie flushed and set her teeth to keep from responding to the jab. 'It offered better possibilities than secretarial work did,' she said quietly. 'In this town, there aren't many choices, even with a college degree.'

'But you didn't stay to get yours. You quit school.'

'You've been doing your homework.' You've been spying on me, she thought. What else does he know?

'Jake McDonald was quite happy to fill me in.' He added thoughtfully, 'All that screaming you did about how important your degree was, and then you gave it up anyway. I wonder why.'

'I don't owe you any explanations, Jordan.'

'Perhaps you don't,' he said softly. 'All that was over long ago. And yet—last night you were wearing the earrings I bought you.'

She was tired of playing games. 'Was I?' she said coolly. 'I'm afraid I'd forgotten where they came from. To what do I owe the honour of this visit?'

His eyebrows went up. 'Weren't you listening last night? I want to buy a house, Stephanie. The Chamber of Commerce president says you're the best real estate person in town.'

'Look, no one would be upset if you ignored his advice. You don't have to—'

'I understand that an agent is a necessity, since the local laws don't allow sale signs to be posted.'

'That's true. But it doesn't have to be me!' Stephanie snapped.

'Don't you want to sell me a house, Stephanie?'

'No. I'd just as soon pretend that you weren't even here in town. And I don't know why you want me—' She broke off, fighting the waves of embarrassed colour that threatened to swamp her. She hadn't planned to state it quite that way.

'I want you—' He paused deliberately, running his eyes over her trim figure in jeans and sweater, a few stray leaves clinging here and there. Stephanie shivered under his gaze as though it were a physical touch. 'I only deal with the best,' he continued quietly. 'Tony Malone has that reputation. And I want you because I'd rather have you working for me than against me. I'm no fool, Stephanie.'

'Well, this time you're out of luck.' Stephanie bent to retrieve her rake, and started stuffing the scattered piles of leaves into a big rubbish bag.

He took the bag out of her hands and held it so it was easier to fill. 'What would you say if I told you that I've already talked to your boss this morning, and he was delighted at the idea of you devoting yourself exclusively to my business?'

Stephanie finished filling the bag. She was a little breathless by then, and she was uneasily aware that it was not from the exertion. She reached for another bag. 'I'd say that my fiancé—' she put careful emphasis on the word '—trusts you a great deal more than I do,' she said finally.

'And where does trust come into it?' he asked, as if surprised.

'I'll talk to Tony. I'm sure he'll understand why I would prefer not to do business with you.'

'You might be surprised,' Jordan said silkily. 'You see, it isn't simply a matter of a house for me, Stephanie. I'll be bringing twenty or thirty key people with me when we're ready to open the factory. Most of them will buy houses, and if I'm pleased with your work, then of course I'll recommend that they come to see you, too.'

'You told Tony that?' she whispered.

'Of course.' He seemed rather excited by the possibility. Come now, Stephanie, what's the problem? Surely you don't believe that I have any plans to seduce you? If that's what you think, my dear, you have a very mistaken notion of yourself. You're still pretty, yes —but irresistible?' He shook his head.

It was a calculated insult, and Stephanie gritted her teeth to keep from striking back. The plastic bag ripped under her nails. She turned away from him to pick up her rake, and when she spoke again her voice was tightly controlled.

'Get off my property, Jordan,' she told him. 'Get lost, and don't come back. You aren't my husband any more, and I don't have to put up with this kind of treatment.'

He didn't seem to have heard her. His gaze was focused on something beyond her, and raw fear touched Stephanie's veins as she turned to see what he was looking at.

Katie had just come around the corner of the house. She was dragging her plastic rake, and she came straight to Stephanie, but she was looking at the stranger instead, her eyes wide with curiosity.

'I found my rake, Mommy,' she confided, and dropped it at Stephanie's feet.

'Mommy?' Jordan repeated. There was a hard edge to his voice.

Katie didn't seem to notice it. 'That's a nice car,' she said, looking up at Jordan with wide eyes. 'Is it yours?'

Jordan nodded. 'Yes, it's mine. What is your name?'

Katie's hand crept into Stephanie's. 'Katie Kendall,' she said shyly. 'Can I have a ride in your car some day?'

Stephanie could see the fury building in Jordan's face. She bent over the child and said, quickly, 'Katie, run over to Julie's house, please, and ask her mother if I can borrow an egg and—and a cup of baking soda, please. All right? Hurry!' It was an odd request, odd enough that she hoped the woman would get the message and keep Katie safely inside until Jordan had gone.

Katie looked puzzled, but she trotted off, pleased to be useful.

'Why did you send her off?' Jordan asked, between gritted teeth.

Stephanie waited till the child was out of earshot. 'Because no one has ever frightened that child, and I'm not going to let you be the first.'

'I just wanted to talk to her.'

Stephanie took a step back, away from the anger that blazed in his eyes. 'I'm sorry if it came as a shock,' she began.

He started to laugh, but there was no humour in him. 'A shock? I'll say it's a shock! So that's why you kept my name! Who was he, Stephanie—your daughter's father?'

She was stunned, speechless, at the accusation.

'No wonder you wouldn't come with me when I got that job offer. No wonder you were so anxious to get a divorce—'

'No!' Her denial was low and hoarse. 'She's your daughter, Jordan—'

'I suppose you're going to tell me that the pills didn't work,' he said bitterly. 'Well, isn't that a coincidence?'

'The last month we were together, I was so upset I forgot to take them half the time,' she admitted. 'They're not guaranteed, you know. And that's when Katie—' Her voice trailed off. In her horridest nightmares, she had never considered this—that Jordan would deny Katie.

It's just as well, she told herself. If he doesn't think she could be his, then he'll leave us both alone.

'I'm leaving town tomorrow,' he said, curtly. 'I have some details to clear up before I'm ready to move. I'll be back Monday. I want to start looking at houses then.'

'Find yourself another agent,' she said.

His smile was vicious. 'If you insist, my dear. Of course, if you refuse, I could tell your fiancé a few things about you. I'm certain that you'd rather maintain the fiction that Katie—that was her name?—is mine.'

'Her name is Kathleen Anne Kendall,' Stephanie said, with bitter emphasis on the last word.

His face darkened. 'Keep up that pretence,' he said, 'and you might tempt me to go after my legal rights.'

'I'm not asking anything from you! Just leave Katie and me alone, Jordan!'

'Beware,' he warned, 'or you might get more than you bargained for, Stephanie.'

The threat hung unspoken in the air between them.

'What about it, Stephanie?' he said. 'Do we deal? Or—'

She was stunned. She had expected that seeing Katie would be the end of his wish to do business with her. Instead, he would use Katie against her—

The silence was a fog that had descended, surrounding them. Then, finally, through a throat so painfully tight that her voice was only a whisper, Stephanie said, 'What kind of a house do you want, Jordan?'

He looked thoughtful. 'I really don't know,' he said. 'I guess I'll have to look at everything in town.' He got into the Lincoln and slammed the door.

Stephanie swallowed hard. 'Do you mean that you will actually trust me?' she said. 'Aren't you afraid that I'll steer you wrong—talk you into buying an unsound house?'

He smiled grimly. 'I hope you do,' he said, and his voice was harsh. 'Because I'll have your licence revoked so fast you won't know what happened. Right now, it would be a pleasure!'

The rest of the day was a blur. Stephanie knew that she had finished raking leaves, because the bags were there on the kerb for the refuse collectors. But she didn't remember doing it.

Late that night, she gave up on trying to sleep. The nightmares that haunted her were too awful to be faced even in the light. She did not want to sleep again, and invite them back.

She glanced in at Katie, peacefully sprawled across her bed with her favourite blanket around her shoulders. The three-storey dolls' house that formed the headboard of her bed cast a long shadow across the bare floor. Katie was safe, and she would be all right. Surely that night-mare would not come true, she told herself. Jordan would go to great lengths to punish Stephanie, but surely he would not hurt an innocent child just to get revenge.

Stephanie brewed a cup of tea and sat down in the little dining nook to drink it. It had been her mother's remedy for all evils, and she found herself going back to it like a magic potion now. As she had in that earlier time, when her marriage had been crumbling under her feet . . .

They had known each other for only a few months before their sudden marriage. Passion, once ignited, had burned steadily higher, and the flames—instead of consuming all their differences—had merely concealed them.

Stephanie's parents had seen the problems, she thought regretfully now, but there had been no time, and she had not been willing to listen to them. She and Jordan had both been so young, so immature, so self-centred, that they had been doomed from the beginning. As an only child, Stephanie had never had to think of anyone but herself. And Jordan's mother had died while he was still a child. He had learned early that unless he took care of himself, no one would.

It had been understandable, what had happened to them. She could see it now, the flaw that had been fatal to their marriage. Compromise was foreign to them both. So long as their needs were met, they were content together, but the instant that their paths diverged, there was no bending.

Their marriage had limped along for several months, held together only by their passion. In bed, it seemed, and nowhere else, they could forget selfishness. There, they could nurture and shelter each other.

But the effort had cost them, and the distance between them was already growing by the time Jordan had been offered the job that to him was the culmination of a long-sought dream. It was a chance to join a fledgling company, one with room for new ideas and ambitious gambles.

To Stephanie it was a death sentence. The company was based in a tiny town, hundreds of miles from the nearest university. She could not finish her education there; she could do nothing but be Jordan's wife.

That might not have been so bad, she thought, now, as she sipped her cooling tea, if the job had offered security, enough money to live comfortably, a steady paycheque. But the same chances that Jordan was so eager to take had panicked Stephanie. She had been unwilling to trust his instincts, his self-confidence. How would they live? What would they do if the company failed? And so she had wanted him to refuse the offer so she could stay at the university until she got her degree and they could move on together. It made perfect sense to her, to wait until they had the security of her job to fall back on.

She had tried, with every weapon at her command, to keep him with her. The passion was still there, but it was empty, no longer all-powerful. And in the end, he had refused to stay with her, and he had gone.

And then her choices had been at an end, for there was her baby to consider. Her education had been sacrificed after all, and she had come back to this little town, where security was easier to find and support from her parents had helped her find her way.

But she had never regretted her refusal to follow Jordan. If he didn't love me enough to consider my wishes, she thought now, then the baby would have made no difference. There would just have been three of us, instead of two, to worry about if the company failed.

Though apparently the company hadn't failed, she thought drily, remembering the brand new car Jordan had been driving. Or if it had, he had landed on his feet once again, and found another opportunity. Or perhaps he had merely found a compliant banker to loan him the money to make a good appearance in this new town.

Jordan has nine lives, she thought. And if I'm not careful, he will outlast me.

Katie, she thought, and fear tugged at her. Now that he has come back into our lives, what will he do to us?

CHAPTER FOUR

THE morning was crisp and cool, ideal weather for sleeping late. Stephanie herself had grumbled about getting out of bed, so she couldn't say much when Katie decided to throw a tantrum as Stephanie was getting dressed.

But eventually their morning routine was accomplished, though Stephanie was running late when she came into the office. Surely, she thought, Jordan wouldn't be around till later in the day. Nevertheless, she breathed a sigh of relief when she glanced around the outer office and found only Susan, the other sales agent, there.

'Is Tony in?' Stephanie asked as Susan put the telephone down and pushed her appointment book away.

'Yes, but he's on the phone—' The bell rang again under her hand, and she said, 'The darn thing has been going crazy all morning.'

'Why on earth?'

'Check the front page of the newspaper,' Susan recommended briefly. 'Everybody in town has a house for sale, now that there might be a market.'

Stephanie picked up the paper. It was an idle gesture; she already knew what she would find there.

The sale of the McDonald plant was big news for this small community. There were pictures—of Jake McDonald, of Jordan, of the plant. There was even a picture of a robot—and what that was doing on the front page was beyond Stephanie. She sat down at her desk, still wearing her outdoor jacket, and started to read.

She had got only a few paragraphs into the article when Tony's door opened. 'Why don't you take your coat off and stay a while?' he asked irritably. 'You're late again, Stephanie.'

She glanced up. 'Katie didn't want to go to preschool this morning.'

He frowned. 'Katie needs to learn that her wishes are not the most important things in the world.'

That was true, Stephanie had to admit. 'I think she might be coming down with a cold.'

He rolled his eyes. 'I suppose that means that you'll have to take a day off to stay home and coddle her.' He didn't give her a chance to answer. 'What did you think of the Anderson house?'

Her irritation was forgotten in a rush of pleasure at the memory of the house. 'It's beautiful, Tony. It would be perfect for us.'

His eyebrows arched skyward. 'For us?' he said, and his tone oozed disbelief. 'Just where do you think we can come up with that kind of money, Stephanie? That house is listed for twice the amount we've been planning to spend!'

'But I thought—'

'You thought what? That we'd find the money growing on trees somewhere so you can live like a queen? No, Stephanie. Sell the Anderson house, and we'll devote the entire commission towards our housing fund.'

Yet another fund for her to contribute to? Of course, she reminded herself, Tony was also saving towards this expensive purchase, by devoting a large percentage of his brokerage fees to the fund. And after all, the house would belong to both of them; it was only fair that she help pay for it.

'I thought you meant that I was to look at it as a possible home for us,' she said finally. Her voice was soft, husky, apologetic.

'Don't be ridiculous,' Tony said tartly. 'I asked you to inspect it—not to fall in love with it. Be sure you show it to Kendall today, by the way. He might like it, and it would certainly be nice to sell it without any investment in advertising.'

He closed his office door with a bang.

Time to get to work, Stephanie thought. He'd made that perfectly obvious. She put the newspaper aside reluctantly, hung her coat up, and settled the collar of her dark blue blazer. Her copper-coloured hair lay satin-smooth over the frilly neckline of her white blouse.

Susan had overheard most of the argument. She turned her chair around and sat for a moment watching as Stephanie fought to control her temper. Finally, she said, with a fond note in her voice, 'Why do you put up with him, Stephanie?'

'Nobody's perfect, Susan.'

'No—but I've seen some who come a whole lot closer than Tony Malone. Why are you ruining your life with him? Is it because you don't think you can do any better?'

'I don't compare him to anyone else.'

Susan muttered something under her breath. Then she said, 'Do you know, in the months that you've been engaged, I've never heard you say anything about loving Tony?'

'That goes without saying.'

'Doesn't that tell you something?' There was a long silence, and then Susan added gently, 'I've been selling real estate out of this office for ten years, and no woman ever took that skinflint seriously until you came along. I think it scares him—'

'Perhaps you're in the wrong field, Susan. You're verging on psychiatry now, not real estate.' Stephanie's voice was taut. Having her romantic associations analysed was the last thing she needed today!

'Sorry,' Susan said. She didn't sound regretful in the least. She turned back to her telephone as it rang again.

It was Susan's day to stay in the office and handle all of the walk-in customers, but she was still on the phone a few minutes later when an expensively dressed woman in her mid-fifties came in, so Stephanie rose to greet her, a bit reluctantly. Hallie McDonald had never been one of her favourite people. Too bad the woman didn't have the charm and warmth her husband did.

'Good morning, Mrs McDonald,' she said, trying to be cheerful. 'Surely you aren't in the market for a house?'

Jake McDonald's wife laughed. 'No, Stephanie. And we're not planning to sell ours, either, though there is a new young man in town who seemed to like it very much.' She managed a girlishly coy look.

So Jordan was trying to buy the McDonald house, as well as the factory. Stephanie wasn't surprised. She fully expected that he would keep her occupied with his search for a house until he tired of the game, and then he would either purchase precisely what he wanted with no help from Stephanie, or he would buy no house at all. If he did end up with a house, he would take delight in preventing her from receiving a commission on the sale. And if he could keep her so busy in the meantime that she had no time for her other customers, that would be icing on the cake of his revenge.

But Tony couldn't see what was happening, Stephanie fumed. He only saw the carrot that had been dangled under his nose—thirty extra commissions on homes sold in the next year. He hadn't even considered the possibility that it was all a bluff. And without Tony's backing, she couldn't even fight Jordan—she was stuck in this awful tangle.

But all that was beside the point; right now she had a customer. 'Is there something I can do for you, Mrs McDonald?'

'I stopped in to ask you, Stephanie, if you would help this year with the Tour of Homes.'

Stephanie was startled. The annual tour of a few of the fanciest houses in town was a charity benefit, but it was also one of the leading society events of the year, and the town's most illustrious matrons were the organisers of the show. Stephanie's involvement in previous years had never gone further than buying a ticket. 'Why me?' Stephanie asked bluntly. If Mrs McDonald was inviting her to take part because of Jordan coming to town, she thought, she wasn't going to be getting the value she expected!

'It isn't till spring, you know, but we're already planning the event. We're having trouble convincing people to open their homes to the public, even when it's in a good cause.' Mrs McDonald shook her head disdainfully.

The woman still hadn't come to the point, Stephanie thought. She knew darned well that she wasn't being asked to put her little house on the Tour of Homes!

'It's an honour to be chosen,' Mrs McDonald fretted, 'and I just don't understand why people won't make a contribution that means so much to the community, and to the charities that we support.'

Honour be damned, Stephanie thought irreverently. It's a nuisance to have five hundred people trailing through your house gawking. 'What are you asking me to do, Mrs McDonald?' she asked warily.

She was rewarded with a glowing smile. 'You talk to so many people who own the really elegant homes here in town, Stephanie, and if you could just persuade two or three of them to be on the tour—I have a list here—'

Stephanie shook her head. 'I'm afraid I couldn't do that, Mrs McDonald. It would conflict with doing my job properly.'

'Oh.' The woman seemed startled, but she recovered herself quickly. 'Well, of course I understand. By the way, my dear, your handsome husband is going to cut quite a path through this town,' she added with a just-between-us smile.

'My ex-husband,' Stephanie corrected through stiff lips. 'We were divorced more than four years ago.'

'Pardon me. My mistake,' Mrs McDonald cooed, but Stephanie thought that she looked just a little triumphant. 'I'm so sorry you can't help us, dear.' And she was gone.

Stephanie shook her head. 'Why do I feel as if I was just manipulated for no good purpose?' she asked Susan. 'Mrs McDonald wasn't upset that I wouldn't do her dirty work on the Tour of Homes, so I wonder what she really wanted.'

Susan looked thoughtful. 'Was Jordan Kendall really your husband?' She reached for the paper. 'This Jordan Kendall?'

'A very long time ago, yes.'

'And now you're engaged to Tony Malone?' Susan shook her head sadly. 'What is the world coming to? As for Mrs McDonald—I think she got what she wanted.' Susan looked down at Jordan's photograph, and then thoughtfully up at Stephanie as she tossed the newspaper back on to the desktop. 'As I recall, the McDonalds have a daughter.'

'Of course they do. Tasha and I were in the same class at school—before her mother sent her out east to boarding school, that is.'

'Have you seen her lately?'

'No. She doesn't spend much time in this town any more. But what does that have to do with anything?'

'Are you dense, Stephanie? They protected that girl from the time she was a baby, because no one around here was good enough for a McDonald.'

'And they've decided Jordan is, and she was checking to be certain that he's available? I wish them luck—if they land Jordan, they'll discover soon enough that he's no prize.' She turned to flip through the listings of houses for sale, refreshing her memory before she took Jordan out to look them over.

'Oh, I don't know,' Susan murmured. 'That's a nice car he drives.'

'Right. But I wouldn't bet on who owns it,' Stephanie returned. She thumped the newspaper with her knuckle, right on top of Jordan's photograph. She wished she dared do it in person; he deserved far more than a punch in the nose.

And stop thinking that way, she warned herself. She had to do business with the man, there was no way out of that. She had better get her temper under control, for she had never known Jordan to lose his. When irritated, he just got more icily dangerous. It made him a formidable foe.

So she put that dark, brooding face out of her mind and started to calculate what the mortgage payments on the Anderson house would add up to.

Tony came out of his office. 'Where's the newspaper?' he demanded.

Stephanie pushed it across to him, and he turned to the stock market figures. 'Dammit,' he yelped. 'Who cut a section out of the middle of the American Exchange?'

'I did,' Susan admitted readily. 'There was a coupon for fifty cents off a pound of coffee on the other side, and the way you are about the cost of office supplies, I figured you'd appreciate getting a bargain.'

Tony's jaw clenched. Then he said, with icy politeness, 'Would you mind letting me look at the back of it?'

'Of course you can see it,' Susan said sweetly, and retrieved the coupon from her desk drawer.

Stephanie hadn't been listening. 'Tony,' she said, finishing her last few figures, 'if we used all the profits from my house as a down payment, we could swing the mortgage payments.'

'Are you still thinking that we can afford the Anderson house? Be realistic, Stephanie. You can't possibly calculate how much profit you'll have. There's no telling how far we'll have to come down from the asking price.'

'But we could manage it! Look here—' She handed him the sheet of paper. 'We could at least make an offer contingent on the sale of my house—'

Tony was shaking his head. 'Nope. Don't spend it till you have it, that's the only sensible way.'

A deep voice from the doorway chided, 'But that would take all the fun out of living, wouldn't it?'

Jordan had come in, very quietly. Stephanie wondered uneasily just how long he had been standing there, eavesdropping.

'Good morning, Mr Kendall!' Tony was jovial. 'We were just talking about a house that we think would be perfect for you. Stephanie will show it to you this morning.'

'I gathered that she was impressed with it,' Jordan said quietly. 'Shall we go, my dear?'

She tossed a pleading look over her shoulder at Tony, hoping that he would react to the familiarity, that he would reconsider even at this late moment. But he was all smiles as Jordan ushered her out to the Lincoln and opened the passenger door.

'We should probably take my car,' she said, a little breathlessly. 'That way you can really look at the houses—'

Jordan shook his head. 'No, thanks. I remember the way you drive. I wouldn't be looking at anything but the road.'

Stephanie bristled, and then told herself to ignore his jabs. If she lost control of her temper, she gave up any chance of getting out of this situation in one piece. 'I really need some information from you, if we aren't going to waste a lot of time,' she said.

Jordan shrugged. 'I have all day to look.'

'There are two hundred houses for sale in this town,' she snapped. 'It would help me out a great deal to know—oh, how many bedrooms you need, for instance—'

'How many would you recommend? I can only sleep in one at a time.'

'Is this house just for you?'

'If you had asked when I first came to town, I would have told you that I had no family at all. Now, of course, we could get into a quarrel over that question, so I won't comment.'

Stephanie bit her lip. Leave it to him to drag Katie into the conversation, she thought, and continued, with difficulty, 'Do you want a formal dining room? Fireplace? Sauna? Patio?'

'Yes.'

'All of those things?' She scrambled to start making notes.

'It depends on the house, of course. Where do we start?' The engine was purring quietly.

This could take forever, Stephanie wailed inside. Her suspicion that he was only taking up her time was growing with each passing minute.

The first two houses were dismissed from the outside. When he drove past a third one, barely slowing down, Stephanie protested. 'How can you know that you don't want that house when you haven't looked at it?'

'Why waste my time on the interior when I already know that I don't want to live in that neighbourhood?' he countered. 'You might as well get serious about this, Stephanie. Showing me every dump in town will not get rid of me.'

She was indignant. 'That house is not a dump, and if you'd only look at it, Jordan Kendall—'

He turned a cool smile on her. 'Or is it that you're trying to prolong the time we spend together? My dear, I had no idea that you still cared!'

The sarcastic words seemed to tear gashes into her heart. Stephanie bit her lip and battled for control. To let him see that he had hurt her would only encourage him to continue. 'Turn left at the next stop sign,' she said finally.

'Is this one another handyman's delight? If so, spare me. I'm looking for a dream house, Stephanie, not a nightmare.'

'And can you afford what you want?' she jibed. 'Dream houses don't come cheap, Jordan, even in this little town. And I don't want to waste my time showing you what you can't afford to buy.'

'That's a thought,' he murmured. 'But don't fret yourself about my mortgage payments, my dear. I'm perfectly able to lie awake at night worrying about them without your help.'

It was just another way to belittle her, she thought furiously. Jordan had never let worries over money keep him awake at night. She had always been the one who had worried about whether they could pay the rent next month. If anything had disturbed Jordan's sleep, it had been work, or lovemaking—

And that's enough of that, she told herself firmly. To think about the few delicious moments of their marriage was to court disaster.

The car had crept to a halt on the edge of the street, and Jordan had half-turned to watch her. 'Are you thinking about Tony?' he asked.

'Why? And why did you stop?'

'I asked the question because you were blushing. And I stopped because you haven't told me where to go from here.'

'Don't tempt me,' Stephanie muttered. She glanced up the street towards the house she had intended to show him, and changed her mind. He wasn't in the mood to be reasonable right now; she might just as well start at the top and work down. Much as she hated the thought of showing Jordan through the Anderson house—'You know where the McDonalds live, don't you? Drive out towards their house and I'll tell you where to turn off.'

The worst part of it was, she reflected, that Jordan probably could afford to buy the Anderson house. If she and Tony could manage it by scrimping and saving, then Jordan could probably talk his banker out of that much cash over a cup of coffee. It isn't fair, she told herself. All Jordan wants is a roof over his head. He had never cared for architectural style, or interior decoration, or elegance, so long as he was warm and comfortable. The Anderson house would be wasted on him.

'I didn't know there were any slums near the McDonalds' neighbourhood.'

'This is not—' Stephanie caught herself, and clipped the argument off short. 'Wait and see.'

The boulevard was lined by houses set back from the street, with brilliant leaves tumbling from spreading old trees. The sun had peeked out after the early-morning gloom, and the day seemed to have a glow.

'You know,' Jordan said conversationally, 'I've been wondering all weekend about your daughter.'

Stephanie tensed, then forced herself to relax. 'Turn right,' she said.

The car took the corner at speed, effortlessly. 'At first I thought that Tony might be her father. But obviously he's not. He's not much of a man, this fiancé of yours, Stephanie.'

'Oh?' Stephanie was a little breathless. 'For your information, Jordan Kendall, it doesn't take much for a man to be a father. But it takes someone special to be a daddy!'

He was laughing. 'So even you agree that Tony isn't the greatest?'

'That wasn't what I said! I—' She broke off abruptly.

'Where did he buy your engagement ring, by the way? In the gum-ball machine at the coffee shop?'

'The diamond is very high quality,' she said. Her voice was taut.

'Oh, there actually is a diamond in it?' Jordan mocked. 'I'm so sorry—but then I've never looked at the ring with a microscope. Does it turn your finger green if you get it wet?'

Stephanie bit her lip, and then said, with dignity, 'Please stop turning up your nose at Tony. If you remember, you didn't give me an engagement ring at all.'

'If I had,' he countered quietly, 'no one would have had to search to find the diamond.'

'That is beside the point. Here's the house.'

The Lincoln paused at the foot of the driveway. Jordan's hands lay loose across the steering wheel as he studied the Anderson house.

Stephanie drew a long breath. 'It's beautiful, isn't it?

His eyes flicked across her face. 'I suppose so, as houses go.' But Stephanie thought she heard a note in his voice that said he had been impressed, against his will.

'The interior is even prettier,' she promised.

'This is the one you and Tony are looking at?'

She heard the note of speculation in his voice. Her mind was racing. If Jordan thought that by buying this house he could keep it away from her, he just might do it. And once he had bought a house, this aggravation would be over, and she wouldn't have to see him again . . . It would almost be worth giving up the house, to get rid of Jordan.

'We're thinking about it,' she said, keeping her voice carefully neutral. 'It's a beautiful house, and of course I'd like to live in it. But our customers have first choice, of course.'

'I see.' Just those two clipped words, but, Stephanie thought triumphantly, he was looking at the house with definite interest.

Her hand was shaking a little as she unlocked the door. It was so very important that he like this house . . .

He walked through the rooms in silence. Stephanie followed at a distance, intruding as little as possible. She tried to keep her daydreams under control, but she couldn't help imagining herself living in this house, her furniture in the big living room, Katie's toys in the family room, her things and Tony's in the big bedroom with its sloped ceiling—

She could feel herself blushing at the idea, as she stood in the bedroom door. Jordan seemed to feel it, too, for he turned in the centre of the room, one eyebrow raised, to look at her. Stephanie retreated to the hallway.

He followed her downstairs a little later, shaking his head. 'I don't understand,' he said. He leaned against the kitchen worktop, looked around, and shook his head. 'What is so grand about this house?'

'It's a lovely house. And it has most of the things you told me you wanted—fireplace, patio, formal dining room. If you're complaining because it doesn't have a sauna, for heaven's sake—'

'Not at all.'

'Just remember that only about two houses in town have them, and one of them is Jake MacDonald's, which I was told on excellent authority is not for sale.' She was out of breath.

'It has nothing to do with the sauna. But this house does not have a formal dining room,' he disagreed mildly. 'It's a traffic lane between the back door and the kitchen. She's just put a table and chairs in the middle of it.'

Stephanie could see the dining room table from where she was standing. She opened her mouth to argue with him, and then she went to the doorway and really looked.

'You're right,' she said finally, still astonished that he had diagnosed so rapidly a problem that had escaped her. 'I never liked that room as well as the rest. Now I know why—because I had to walk around the furniture all the time.'

Jordan shrugged. 'There must be something about this house that is attractive,' he said, 'but I can't for the life of me imagine what you see in it. So why don't you do your sales pitch, Stephanie?'

'The kitchen, for one,' she said instantly. 'The oak cabinetry and the way the appliances are arranged. It is the ideal floor plan for efficiency.'

He made a noise that might have been assent. 'And what else?'

'The family room. Ideal for children's toys—Oh, well.' She had forgotten that Jordan would be less than interested in facilities for children.

'It's at the wrong end of the house,' he said.

'It's out of the way. What do you mean, wrong end of the house?'

'A family room should be next to the kitchen. Where does your little darling play now?'

'In the middle of the living room,' Stephanie said.

Jordan nodded. 'If you think she will stay by herself when the rest of the family is at the other end of the house, you are a fool. Result, one useless room.'

'Is there nothing that you like about this house?'

'Not much. What's next on your list?'

Stephanie consulted her notebook as the car glided down the drive. At the street, Jordan turned to look back at the Anderson house, gleaming in the sun. Then he shook his head. 'You may have it with my blessing,' he said. 'If your beloved will ante up the cash, that is.'

The vague sneer in his voice was like sandpaper on her nerves. 'Tony is careful with his money,' she agreed, her voice tight. 'Unlike other people I know, who would spend their last dime on steak and then live on rice and beans till the next windfall—'

'Where Tony would settle for an assured diet of hamburger?'

'It's at least steady, and predictable.'

'And dull,' he nodded. 'It's flattering, in a back-handed way, Stephanie.'

'What is?'

'That you've chosen someone so much different from me for your second husband,' he said gently. 'Because you know very well, my dear, that dull is the one thing I never was.'

CHAPTER FIVE

THE alarm on her clock radio shrilled, and Stephanie shot straight up in bed as if a siren had gone off beside her. 'It can't be morning yet,' she wailed, and turned the alarm off. But it was. Another day, another list of houses for Jordan to glance at and reject, probably a new customer lost because Stephanie was out on this wild-goose chase instead of tending to the real business.

They had looked at ten more houses after he had so lightly dismissed the Anderson house. Jordan was proving to be harder to please than any other customer Stephanie had ever dealt with, and her suspicion was growing that, no matter what she showed him, he would not buy.

She had said, in utter frustration at mid-afternoon, 'If I showed you Buckingham Palace, you wouldn't like it!'

Jordan had answered thoughtfully, 'Oh, I don't know. I always wanted to live in a castle.'

Castle, she thought now, resentfully. If he thought he was going to find a castle in this little town, he would be looking for a long time.

Her eyes were burning and watering from lack of sleep, and she rubbed at them fiercely. Her throat was also raw, she noted glumly, and her head felt stuffy. 'Thanks a bunch, Katie,' she muttered. 'You not only picked up a cold at preschool, you had to bring it home to me!' She resolutely pushed the blankets back.

Katie was still asleep, her thumb in her mouth, her rag doll cradled in one arm. Stephanie stood in the doorway of the child's room and watched her sleep for a few minutes. Then she decided to get dressed herself before waking Katie. She wasn't up to another tantrum this morning.

Even a sip of water scraped her protesting throat, and she sneezed a half-dozen times in the two minutes it took to wash her face. Her eyes were reddened and fever-bright in the mirror. 'I'm no fit competition for Jordan this morning,' she muttered. 'I couldn't sell handkerchiefs today, much less houses.' She took her temperature and sighed, then went to call Tony at the office to tell him that she was ill.

Susan answered the phone. 'He isn't in yet, Stephanie, but I'll tell him,' she said sympathetically. 'What are you going to do with Katie?'

Stephanie, who had forgotten about Katie, groaned. It hurt her throat. 'She's still asleep. I'll figure out something.'

'Take care of yourself. Hot chicken soup, aspirin, and tea with honey—'

Stephanie's head was throbbing by the time she got back to bed. The pillow case was cool against her hot cheek, and it was a relief to just lie back and know that she would not have to face anyone all day.

She was dozing an hour later when Katie came in, fresh from sleep, trailing the battered rag doll by the foot. 'Are you going to work, Mommy?' she asked politely.

Stephanie rolled over with a moan. 'No, darling. I'm sick.' She tried to get out of bed, intending to call her mother and ask if she could pick Katie up for the day. But her head hurt too badly for her to move.

Katie, her forehead wrinkled with concern, straightened Stephanie's pillow, smoothed the creases out of the sheet, and helped her to lie down again. 'Go to sleep, Mommy,' she advised.

Stephanie cursed the day that she had decided not to put in a bedside phone. The distance to the living room seemed too much to negotiate right now, no matter how important it was that she talk to her mother. 'I'll call in a little bit,' she muttered.

Katie tiptoed out. 'I close the door so nothing bothers you,' she announced from the hallway.

My little girl is growing up and becoming thoughtful of others, Stephanie noticed. 'You do that, Katie. And if anyone calls, say I'm dying and can't be disturbed.' She buried her head in the pillow again.

Stephanie had always hated being ill. She didn't like having her plans interrupted, and she loathed being idle while much more interesting activities beckoned. Moreover, she had a low pain threshold, and she had never been good at putting up with headaches or other assorted bodily ills.

Part of the problem was that her mother had spoiled her, Stephanie thought dreamily, remembering the days of her childhood illness when her mother had whipped up concoctions to tempt a feeble appetite, played games with her, told her stories to pass the weary hours. Now she was strictly on her own.

She drifted off to sleep, with the remembered scent of steaming chicken soup tempting her nose. When the phone rang a few minutes later, she struggled back to consciousness just long enough to hear Katie say, indignantly, 'Don't you 'sturb my mommy! She's sick!'

'Thatta girl, Katie,' her mother murmured and sank back into her pillow. It had probably been Tony, checking up on where she had left her multiple-listing book, or some such nonsense. It was easier to call her than it was to look for it. Well, Tony could cope by himself today, she told herself firmly. It would be good for him to have to show Jordan through a few houses. Then he might understand the trouble she was having, and how impossible it was that Jordan would ever be satisfied.

But it was too much trouble to stay awake to think about it. Her body was begging for healing sleep, and she let herself drift back towards oblivion.

When the crash came, however, Stephanie's four years of experience in motherhood took over, and she was out of bed and half-way across the living room before her eyes were even open. She paused in the kitchen doorway in horror.

'Kathleen Kendall—' she said, with a threatening note in her voice, and Katie burst into tears.

The child was standing in the middle of the kitchen floor. The coating of flour over her whole body, hair and all, was like a powdering of angel dust. Her tears left clean streaks down her chubby cheeks. Under the flour, she was still wearing her red gingham nightgown, and her hair had tumbled half-way out of the ponytail Stephanie combed it into each night to keep it from tangling. Her feet were bare, and less than six inches from her toes was the reason for the crash—a glass bottle of maple syrup which had shattered on the floor.

'For heaven's sake, Katie, stand still!' Stephanie ordered, with horror in her voice, as she stepped across the spilled flour and plucked her daughter out of the sticky mess.

Katie, scared of the consequences, wailed all the harder. Stephanie set her on the worktop and inspected each bare toe, but the glass shards had done no damage.

Stephanie sighed in relief, and then turned a stern look on her daughter. 'Kathleen, what on earth were you doing?' she quizzed. She reached for a cloth and started to clean the syrup off Katie's feet.

Katie sniffled. 'I was making breakfast in bed for you.'

Stephanie's head had cleared momentarily, during the worst of her concern for Katie, but now it began to pound again. She looked around at the wreckage of the kitchen.

The syrup was the worst of it, but there was more. An egg had rolled off the worktop and splattered, shell and all, across the floor. A half-full glass of orange juice sat in a puddle beside the sink; Katie wasn't expert yet at pouring. And over everything was that fine dusting of flour.

'Pancakes?' Stephanie said drily.

Katie nodded, happy that her mother was so quick to understand. 'I watch you make them,' she volunteered.

Stephanie picked up a mixing bowl and stirred its contents idly. 'And what is this?'

'Cereal,' Katie said. 'But I got too much milk, so I poured it into a big bowl. And then—'

'I see.' Stephanie poured the excess down the drain.

'I was hungry,' Katie admitted.

It sounded like a normal day for Katie. Stephanie knew she should have expected something of the sort to happen. 'Why don't you go call Grandma and ask if you can spend the day with her—all right?'

Katie's face clouded over again. 'I love you, Mommy.'

Stephanie's heart melted. She couldn't stay angry; after all, Katie had the best of intentions. Thank heaven, she thought, that the child hadn't tried bacon and coffee!

'I love you, too, darling. But I'm sick today. Go call Grandma, please, while I clean up the broken glass.' She lifted Katie down and hugged her.

'I don't want to go to Gramma's,' Katie muttered. Then she sniffed and went off slowly, feet dragging, towards the telephone. Two big tears were sliding down her cheeks.

Stephanie started to clean up the mess. Beside the sink was a tray, already neatly laid with silverware and napkin. Beside the coffee cup—it's a good thing I heard her before she got any further, Stephanie thought—was a photograph of a red rose, clipped neatly from the new magazine that had been in yesterday's mail . . .

Katie always had the best of intentions, Stephanie thought. Her tender-hearted child, always looking out for others, always protecting a hungry kitten, always ready to offer her toys . . .

How, Stephanie wondered in astonishment, did two such selfish people as Jordan and I produce such a giving child?

She had picked all of the glass out of the puddle of syrup by the time the doorbell rang. Thank God, she thought, Mother must have taken Katie seriously to have come this quickly. Maybe she'll stick around a little while and take care of me, too . . .

Her head was throbbing. Just being out of bed was enough of an effort, and bending over the sticky puddle was making her feel light-headed. Just a little more, she was telling herself firmly. As soon as you get the puddle cleaned up, you can go back to your comfortable bed.

Katie appeared in the doorway again, twisting the hem of her red gingham nightgown up into a tail.

'Go and get your clothes on,' Stephanie suggested, 'so Grandma can take you home.'

'Gramma isn't here,' Katie said cheerfully.

'Then who rang the—' Stephanie stopped dead. She was at eye-level with the child as she scrubbed up the syrup, and suddenly beside Katie's small bare toes, a pair of large, black leather shoes appeared.

Her gaze trailed reluctantly upward, over grey trousers, a dark blue jacket, a striped silk tie . . . 'Hello, Jordan,' she said weakly. Katie, she thought, my dear and trusting daughter, I'm going to spank you for this! If Jack the Ripper knocked on the door and asked to borrow a carving knife, you would invite him in to take his choice!

She was miserably aware that she had never looked worse in her life. Her eyes were puffy and lined, her hair was flat and tousled, her battered old nightshirt had never been elegant even when new. And she was up to her wrists in a puddle of maple syrup.

Katheleen Kendall, she wailed inside, how could you do this to me?

'Katie was hungry, so she decided to fix breakfast,' she said finally.

Jordan's eyes were icy. 'It is eleven o'clock in the morning,' he pointed out. 'I should think by now you could have stirred yourself to feed her.'

Stephanie's eyebrows arched. 'Well, if it isn't Father Christmas himself,' she said sarcastically. 'I suppose I'd better watch my step or I'll find myself up on a charge of child neglect.'

'Stranger things have happened,' he said coldly. 'She looks like a waif in need of care, that's certain.'

Katie was looking from one to the other of them, a puzzled wrinkle on her forehead. Stephanie supposed that some sort of introduction was in order, but she didn't feel up to making it.

'And to think,' Jordan drawled, 'that this child is so protective of you, when you obviously don't bother to supervise her.'

'Protective?' Stephanie was having trouble making sense of the conversation. She wrung out her cleaning rag and wiped at the floor again. The rag was so sticky by now that she wasn't sure if she was making progress or not.

'Yes. She told me this morning that you weren't to be disturbed, and hung up on me.'

'Oh.' Stephanie's voice was weak. 'It was you on the phone.'

'Yes. They'd told me at the office that you were ill, which I had trouble believing. I dropped by to see for myself whether you were hiding out—though I must admit you're not exactly the picture of blooming health today.'

'Two points for your perceptiveness.' She got to her feet wearily, rinsed the syrup off her hands, and reached for another rag.

Suddenly the room was spinning around her. She reached out for something to hold on to, and her hand closed on emptiness. Everything looked orange, and she thought, horrified, I'm going to faint, and he'll never believe I didn't do it on purpose.

Jordan's arm was like a steel brace around her, keeping her from falling. And it was just about as personal, too, Stephanie thought. She would have pulled away from him, but she was too grateful for the support.

'Sorry,' she said breathlessly, as some of the dizziness passed. 'I got up too suddenly, I guess. Thanks—it could have been nasty if I'd collided with the stove on my way down.' She was babbling, she knew, but she couldn't stop herself.

He was frowning, and when she tried to pull away, his arm tightened. 'You're running a fever,' he said. 'You're burning up.'

'Congratulations. I told you I was sick.' She wouldn't look at him. 'Katie, did you call Grandma?'

Katie shook her head slowly, and then took her thumb out of her mouth. 'Don't want to go to Gramma's,' she said.

'You're going anyway. Jordan, I'm perfectly fine now. Would you let go of me?'

'You belong in bed,' he said. His hand was still firm on her arm.

'A wonderful idea. Why don't you clear out so I can get there?'

Instead, he picked her up. 'You still don't weigh enough to bother with,' he said under his breath as he carried her into the hallway.

Stephanie's throat was tight. The memory of other times when he had held her like this was doing funny things to her breathing. The scent of his aftershave brought back those times when he had held her, cuddled her, made love to her—Don't be ridiculous, Stephanie, she told herself. 'The back bedroom,' she said, determined not to lose her dignity.

He put her down and stayed still for a moment,

leaning over her in the big bed. For just an instant, Stephanie thought she saw something flare in his eyes. Then he straightened the blankets around her shoulders with calm efficiency, and the ice was back in his eyes.

It was only your imagination, she told herself. Your foolish, stupid imagination. 'Katie!' she called.

'I'll take her over to your parents' house,' Jordan volunteered.

Stephanie gritted her teeth. It was almost more than she could bear, having to accept favours from him. But there was little she could do about it. She certainly wasn't going to get out of bed again.

'Thank you,' she said stiffly.

'It has nothing to do with you. I want to be sure Katie is taken care of,' he said, and left the room.

'That's certainly a switch,' she muttered. The pillow was cool against her cheek, and she was too miserable to worry about Jordan's sudden change of tone. He was only out to prove that she was a fool anyway, she told herself. And she was giving him the perfect opportunity.

Katie trailed in a few minutes later. 'I get to ride in his car,' she announced.

Stephanie sat up with an effort to help fasten zippers and buttons. 'Yes, dear. I know.'

'Who is he?' Katie asked.

It was a puzzler. Stephanie bit her lip and thought about it. She could scarcely introduce him as Mr Kendall, and Jordan was not likely to react positively about being called Daddy, however true it was.

'Why don't you ask him what he'd like to be called?' she said finally. It was only fair to pass the problem on to him, after all; it really wasn't Stephanie's to answer. Katie looked her over thoughtfully and then kissed her goodbye.

Stephanie sank gratefully back on to her pillow again, but she wasn't to be left in peace. A few minutes later Jordan was back with a mug that steamed delightfully, a tall glass full of orange juice and chipped ice, and a bottle of aspirin. 'It's only soup from a can, but it will help your throat,' he said brusquely. 'Get some sleep.' He was gone before she could bring herself to thank him.

She heard the front door close on Katie's chatter as she took her first grateful swallow of the hot soup. It did soothe her throat, and by the time it was gone she was deliciously sleepy again.

It was dark when she woke. It took a minute to orientate herself, and then she stretched, to find that the stiffness and muscle pain were gone. 'It's been years since I slept all day,' she said to the silent house, feeling just a little guilty. Her head was still stuffy, but the pounding ache was gone and she felt almost human again.

She pushed the blankets back and gingerly tried her feet. The dizziness had passed with rest, and a quick hot shower and fresh pyjamas completed her restoration.

And she was beginning to feel hungry. She found the rest of the soup in a pan in the refrigerator, and put it on to heat. The kitchen floor, she noticed, was sparkling clean. Thoughtful of Jordan, she admitted, to get rid of the mess for her.

I'll call Mom and ask her to bring Katie home, she decided, and then I'll have another cup of soup, watch a little television, and go back to bed as soon as Katie goes to sleep.

It sounded like a wonderful plan. Stephanie laughed at herself. Television and early to bed—'You're getting old, Stephanie Kendall,' she accused, and was astonished when her voice emerged as a hoarse croak.

Her mother was horrified. 'Stephanie, you sound awful!'

'Actually, I'm much improved from this morning. I think I'm up to coping with Katie now, if you'd like to bring her home.'

There was a sudden dead silence on the other end of

the line, and then Anne Daniels said slowly, 'Katie isn't here, Steph.'

Stephanie's hand clenched on the edge of the table as dread clutched her heart. 'What do you mean?' she asked breathlessly. Dad must have taken her downtown, she told herself frantically, or she's across the street playing with her friend—that's all Mother means.

'I haven't seen Katie all day. I assumed that you'd taken her to the day-care centre. You—Stephanie, you didn't send her to walk over here, did you?' There was horror in Anne's voice.

'Of course not, Mom. Jordan said he'd drop her off—' Oh, my God, she thought. After what he said this morning about Katie being mistreated, how could she have trusted him? He'd probably delivered the child to the local welfare office. By now Katie could have been placed in a foster home—

Hold it, she ordered herself. Don't panic yet.

'I went to lunch with the girls,' Anne fretted. 'But I was only gone a little while, and I've been right here all the rest of the day. I don't understand . . .'

'It's all right, Mom. How were you to know?' Stephanie felt a little strange about comforting her mother, when right now all she herself wanted to do was to sit down and burst into tears.

You idiot, how could you have trusted him? she berated herself. But in the meantime, there was no sense in her mother worrying about it. 'It was about lunchtime when they left here,' she said. 'You must have been gone, and he—' But what would he have done? Where would he have taken Katie?

'Shall I come over?'

Stephanie tried to laugh. 'Heavens, no, that's not necessary.' She was trying to reassure herself as well. Whatever he might have done, Jordan would not have hurt Katie. Would he? She could call the police . . . She shuddered at the very thought.

Car lights swept across the front of the house, and Stephanie pulled the curtain aside. The wave of relief that swept over her when she recognised Jordan's Lincoln was so intense that it threatened to choke her. She waited another instant, watching as the passenger door opened and Katie climbed out—

'It's all right,' she said. 'He's brought her home.'

Anne sighed. 'Thank God. And if you ever scare me like that again, Stephanie—'

Katie was banging on the front door, so Stephanie said a hasty goodbye and went to open it.

She knelt on the doormat beside Katie, who flung herself into her mother's arms. It felt so good to hold this little bundle of squirming energy, Stephanie thought. I'd forgotten how precious she really is.

Katie's words were coming so fast that they tumbled over each other. 'We played in the park and we fed the squirrels and we watched them practise football—'

'The squirrels?' Stephanie asked, a little dazed by the cascade of words.

'No, silly. The football players. And a goose almost bit me and we saw a castle and Daddy pushed me high in the swings—higher than the clouds,' she chattered.

So he's Daddy now, Stephanie thought, and wanted to brush away the tears that threatened to form. She felt as if something very important had vanished today—as if Katie's babyhood had irretrievably disappeared.

The child's eyes were bright and her cheeks rosy from the chilly air. 'And we ate hamburgers and I brought you a flower 'cause you're sick—' A long-stemmed red rose was carefully transferred from Katie's chubby fist to Stephanie's hand.

She looked up at Jordan. 'You shouldn't have,' she chided softly.

He didn't pretend to misunderstand. 'She picked out the rose. It wasn't my idea.'

'But it was your money.'

'And look what Daddy got me,' Katie plunged on. She twisted around in Stephanie's arms. 'Daddy! Where's Miranda Panda?'

'Still in the car,' Jordan said solemnly. 'Remember? We wanted to be sure your mommy was awake before we brought her in.'

'Well, get her,' Katie dictated.

'Kathleen!' Stephanie protested. 'Where are your manners?'

Jordan raised an eyebrow, and Katie flashed her dimples at him and said, 'Please?'

'That's better, Peanut,' he said, and went out to the car.

The nickname, as much as the fond, teasing note in his voice, frightened Stephanie. Her mother had been right after all, she was thinking. He had obviously changed his mind about Katie today.

He was back in a moment with a stuffed panda that was at least four feet tall. 'Miranda Panda,' Stephanie said, with foreboding.

Katie tugged the enormous bear down the hall and into her room, chattering to herself all the way.

The sudden silence in the living room was deafening. Stephanie was getting light-headed again. 'I don't know how to thank you for taking care of her today,' she said finally. 'It's obvious that she enjoyed herself.'

'So did I.' It was clipped, cool.

Stephanie wished fretfully that he would just go away. She put a hand to her head, which had started to ache again.

'Have you eaten anything?' he asked abruptly.

She had forgotten the pan of soup on the stove. She shook her head, and then wished that she hadn't. He made no comment, but he went straight to the kitchen.

A few minutes later he was back with another mug of steaming soup and a plate of crackers.

'How fearfully boring for you,' Stephanie said, trying

to pass it off lightly. 'Babysitting, and taking care of an invalid—'

'Nothing of the kind. I'm just trying to get you back in shape, because I found the house I want to buy today.'

'Which one?'

'Oh, it's nothing that you showed me. I want you to get busy on it tomorrow.'

'Oh, you do?' Stephanie's tone was dry. 'And how did you conclude that it's for sale? Clairvoyance?'

'Everything is for sale at the right price. Besides, it's empty, and it obviously has been for some time.'

Katie came back out of her room, wearing her favourite pyjamas with the ducks on them. Stephanie was so astounded that she almost dropped her cup. Was this the same child who fought bedtime in a nightly ritual, who denied that the clock could be right?

'I'm sleepy,' she said, and yawned. 'G'night, Mommy. G'night, Daddy. Will you tuck me in?'

Stephanie drank her soup and felt very left out as she sat in the living room and listened to the rise and fall of Jordan's voice as he read a bedtime story. But eventually the lights were turned off and he returned, to stretch out in a chair with a sigh.

'I understand why you needed help today,' he said, and yawned. 'She's an exhausting job.'

'I gather that you've come to terms with fatherhood,' Stephanie said coolly.

There was a gleam in Jordan's dark blue eyes. 'You must admit that it came as a bit of a shock,' he said. 'But yes, I'm now resigned to the idea that Katie is mine.'

He didn't sound resigned, Stephanie thought. In fact, he sounded vaguely threatening.

'The baby sampler in her room helped to convince me,' he added. 'I doubt that you would go to that much trouble for a practical joke.'

Stephanie remembered the sampler. Her mother had made it when Katie was born, and included all the pertinent details in microscopic needlepoint, down to Katie's weight and length. And parents, Stephanie reminded herself.

'Not to mention the physical evidence,' he went on. 'She certainly didn't get that dark hair from you.'

Stephanie absently twisted an auburn curl around her finger. 'It sounds as if you had a wonderful day,' she said. 'Just don't get any notions about your future with Katie —because things are quite comfortable as they have been.'

'Comfortable for whom?' Jordan asked genially.

'Well, I have no intention of changing anything.'

'And just what kind of changes do you think I have in mind?' His voice had grown cold. 'I'm certainly not planning to take up where we left off; I have problems enough without adding you to them, Stephanie.'

She should have expected something of the sort, she thought, but it stung anyway.

'You're the one who's planning to be married,' he continued. 'That seems like change enough for anyone, especially Katie. The only thing I want is to see her now and then—that's little enough to ask, isn't it?'

Stephanie was silent. She couldn't deny him the right to see Katie, that was sure. She would only buy herself trouble if she tried. 'You don't have to hang around now that Katie is in bed,' she pointed out.

'I'm waiting till she's settled down, so she doesn't disturb you.' Jordan put his head back and closed his eyes, as if daring her to disagree. He let the silence drag out. Then he said, 'I'll be busy at the plant tomorrow, so you'll be on your own with the house.'

Thank God you'll be busy, Stephanie wanted to say. 'Oh, yes, the house. Where did you find this dream cottage?'

He frowned. 'It's hardly a cottage. Does the name Whiteoaks mean anything to you?'

Stephanie repeated it, under her breath. Then she

started to laugh. 'You must be joking! The big, sprawl-ing house surrounded by all the overgrown hedges and dead trees and weeds?'

'With the tower,' Jordan agreed, 'and the tile roof, and the wrought iron gate with the name on it.'

'It's stood there empty for years,' she said. 'It's tied up in an estate, and the heirs can't agree on what to do with it. It is not for sale, Jordan.'

He smiled. 'You're too modest, my dear. I'm sure that you can persuade the owners to reconsider.'

'Jordan, don't be ridiculous!'

He yawned, stretched, stood up. 'I must get some sleep,' he said, as if to himself. 'I have an appointment with my attorney in the morning. It should be very interesting to see what he's found out.'

'Oh?' Stephanie didn't know why that simple state-ment should frighten her, but it did.

Jordan smiled. 'Yes. He's doing some research for me. If you remember, my dear, our divorce papers state specifically that there are no children involved. You lied to the court, Stephanie, and it seems that now there might be all kinds of complications.' His voice was silky. 'Perjury isn't a pretty thing, my dear.'

'I didn't lie! I didn't know I was pregnant when I filed those papers . . .' Her voice trailed off. What could he do about it now, anyway, she wondered. It was all over so long ago.

'I wish you'd just go away!' she cried. 'Go away and never come back. I don't ever want to see you again, Jordan—'

His hands were clenched, and his eyes had hardened to blue icicles. For a moment she wondered if he would strike her. She would almost have welcomed the out-burst; at least then he might have seemed human and not this cold, controlled nemesis who was pursuing her, hounding her . . .

But he merely said, very softly, 'Work hard on

Whiteoaks for me, Stephanie. Once I own it, I won't have time to worry about the little things any more. But until then—'

The threat remained unspoken. She watched him drive away, her hand clutched at her throat.

CHAPTER SIX

STEPHANIE showed the Anderson house again the next morning. The prospective buyer loved it. 'I'd take it in a minute,' she confided. 'But my husband has to give his approval too, of course, and he thinks it's too much money.'

Stephanie had walked through the rooms again, trying to pretend that she was the hostess here, displaying her new home to a guest. But the magic was gone. The dining room looked small and cramped to her newly aware eyes, and the family room was inconveniently located. Darn Jordan anyway, she thought crossly, and then reconsidered. It was probably just as well that he had shattered that particular dream. Tony would never have let her buy the Anderson house, and if Stephanie couldn't have it for herself, then it really didn't matter who owned it.

I just wish someone would buy it in a hurry, she thought. She said a polite goodbye to her client and sat in her car in the driveway of the Anderson house for several minutes, wondering how on earth to convince Jordan that Whiteoaks was not for sale.

Because unless she could convince him to give up on it, she didn't even want to think about the consequences.

It was no wonder that she hadn't thought of the house herself as a possible home for Jordan. In the first place, every real estate salesman in town—including Tony —had tried to talk the heirs into selling it three years ago, when old Mrs Barclay had died. Now it had been empty and deserted for so long that even the people who had wanted to buy it then were no longer interested. Eventually everyone in town had given up, assuming that Whiteoaks would stand there on its acres of rolling lawn, quietly mouldering away as the brush and weeds grew up around it and the heirs argued, until someday the bright tile roof would just fall in.

Stephanie hadn't even driven past it in months. I wonder what condition it's in by now, she thought. Perhaps Jordan thinks he can pick it up for a song because it needs so much work.

At least she could go over there and look at it, she decided. Perhaps after a careful examination, she could even convince him to give up this mad idea.

Whiteoaks stood well back from the street, at the end of a row of elegant executive houses. The owners of those houses would be delighted if it was sold, she thought. They probably considered it an eyesore, even though it was off to the side, separated from the well-manicured lawns of its neighbours by a shallow ravine. In the summer, Stephanie remembered, the ravine was full of wild flowers.

She slowed her car to a crawl, but still she could catch only a glimpse of the house itself behind the sagging wrought iron gates. It was well hidden behind its wall of bushes and shrubs; she wondered how Jordan had managed to stumble on to it.

The service entrance was unblocked, and she parked her car near the back door and walked around the sprawling house. As she stood on the weedy front lawn, admiring the brilliance of the red-leafed ivy that had clambered over the walls, she remembered what Katie had said last night about seeing a castle. Yes, Stephanie thought, that was what Whiteoaks looked like. The massive brick structure looked as if it could survive any attack. There was a tower off to one side of the huge carved front door. The door itself resembled a draw-bridge. There was even a flagpole mounted in a ragged flower bed by the main driveway—didn't every honest-to-goodness castle display the colours of its lord and master whenever he was in residence?

'Knowing Jordan,' she muttered snidely, 'I wouldn't be at all surprised if he designs himself a flag!'

Without a key, of course, she could do little more than peer in the dusty casement windows. There must be thousands of panes, she thought. It was a wonder that the neighbourhood kids hadn't decided to use it for target practice.

She suspected that Jordan knew no more about the house than she did, and she wondered how he could be so certain that this was what he wanted. Then she answered her own question—he had said he wanted it simply because he suspected she couldn't get it for him. How pleasant it would be, she thought, if she could arrange a sale, and then Jordan had to back out of buying the house. He would be publicly embarrassed. It was a pleasant thought.

She went back to the office fired with a new resolve. Jordan Kendall was not going to get the best of her, she vowed. She knew a few tricks that she hadn't used yet.

Tony was frowning over the newspaper in the front office, checking out the fluctuations of his chosen stocks. 'I wonder if Robonics stock will be worth buying,' he muttered.

'That's a new one on me,' Stephanie said.

'If I can buy it low, and ride it up,' he mused, 'I could make a lot of money. But on the other hand, if it doesn't go over big, it could be a big risk to hold a lot of stock in a new company. I wonder how it will do.'

'If you knew that, you wouldn't be selling real estate. What is Robonics, anyway?'

'It's the company that bought the McDonald plant. Kendall's outfit. Since it's a local firm, it would be easy to keep an eye on, but—'

'See? I told you he wasn't working for himself,' Stephanie pointed out.

Tony wasn't listening. 'The parent company is showing strong. The original owners are all millionaires, but that doesn't mean they can do it again. I just don't know about this new venture.' Tony sounded fretful, almost whiny.

'Which new venture?' Stephanie wasn't particularly interested, but if Tony wanted to talk about the stock market, it would be impossible to move him on to another subject.

'Building robots. Didn't you know that's what they're going to do at the McDonald plant?'

'How should I know?' Now she was definitely interested. So Jordan was up to his neck in robots, now. Well, trust Jordan to be in on something that ordinary people knew nothing about!

Tony sent her a long, hard look, full of suspicion. 'If he hasn't told you about his business,' he asked pointedly, 'then what do you and your ex-husband find to talk about to while away the hours?'

'Come on, Tony. Don't be ridiculous. So he's building robots?'

'Don't you even read the newspaper? Haven't I told you often enough how important it is that you know everything you can about a client?'

'Yes, you've told me. And speaking of that, have you run a credit check on Jordan?'

Tony scowled. 'No. Why should I?'

'So that we aren't all embarrassed if he turns out to be a pauper.'

'Paupers don't drive Lincolns.'

'Maybe it's a company car,' Stephanie said sweetly. 'So what's the deal with the robots? Do they really need a plant the size of that one to build toys?'

Tony snorted. 'Hardly toys, Stephanie. Robots are now used to manufacture goods, to search for explosives, to check manholes and sewer pipes where human would be in danger from the poisonous gases— all kinds of things. It could be the wave of the future.'

He nibbled his pen, thinking about it.

'Or it could fall flat,' she reminded. 'Tony, who really owns Whiteoaks? The heirs, I mean. Who are they?'

His eyebrows shot up. 'Stephanie,' he said, in a warning tone. 'I don't know what kind of manipulation you're pulling now, but you can cut it out. I will not be manoeuvred into buying the Anderson house!'

She was bewildered. 'How did we get from Whiteoaks to the Anderson house? All I'm doing is asking questions for a client. Jordan wants to buy Whiteoaks, and I can't talk to the owners unless I know who they are.'

Tony was mollified. 'Oh. It seemed a natural assumption, that it all had something to do with the Anderson house.'

'Why did you jump to conclusions?' She was furious. 'I don't play games like that, Tony. I never have! I'm not crazy enough to try to make you do anything—'

'Because Beth Anderson is one of the four heirs, that's why.'

Stephanie's mouth dropped open. 'You're joking.'

'No. Her mother was a Barclay—some kind of relation to old Mrs Barclay's husband.'

'And the others?' Stephanie pushed the newspaper aside and perched on the corner of her desk.

'Two of them live out of town. They were second cousins of Mrs Barclay—something like that.'

'And the fourth one?'

'Hallie McDonald.'

It took a second for Stephanie to digest that. 'Hallie —do you mean that Mrs Jake McDonald owns Whiteoaks?'

'Only a fourth of it,' Tony corrected.

Stephanie started to laugh. 'It ought to be interesting to see Jordan's face when I tell him this,' she chuckled. 'He thought he was giving me the impossible task, and all the time, Hallie McDonald holds the key to it—'

'That's for sure. She's the one who doesn't want to sell it,' Tony pointed out.

'But why not? She certainly doesn't want to live in it.'

'Search me. She hasn't confided in me. But she obviously doesn't need the money. Even when McDonald's corporation went bust, he was well protected personally. And most of the money is hers, anyway, not his.'

Stephanie found a caramel in her desk drawer, thoughtfully unwrapped it, and put it in her mouth. 'What about Mrs Anderson?' she asked indistinctly.

Tony frowned at her. 'You and Katie,' he muttered. 'You both act four years old sometimes.'

She refused to be upset. 'Think of it as part of my youthful charm, Tony.'

He grunted. 'I don't know how Beth Anderson feels,' he said. 'I haven't talked to her about it in ages, and the quarrel has all been a long time ago.'

'But they have to do something with it some day,' Stephanie pointed out. She stared thoughtfully at the wall.

Tony shrugged. 'Maybe. Maybe not.' He was flipping through the newspaper. 'There's an auction Saturday that looks interesting—want to go?'

'With this cold of mine? I'm not sure I want to stand around outside. And the way Katie hates auctions—'

'I thought perhaps you'd get a sitter so we could enjoy ourselves.'

If Stephanie had thought it over, she wouldn't have said it, but the words popped out before she could stop herself. 'With the percentage you're holding out of my commission cheques, I can't afford to hire a sitter on Saturdays, too, Tony.'

He frowned. 'You seem to find plenty of money to do what you want.'

'I'm certainly not the one who's worrying about which stocks to invest my excess cash in,' she said sweetly.

'Some day you'll thank me,' he said. 'By the time we're ready to buy a house, we'll have a nice little nest egg here.'

'Sometimes I wonder if we'll ever be ready to buy,' Stephanie said. 'What use is a savings account if you can't use it? Saving money is not supposed to be a one-way street, Tony.' He didn't answer, and Stephanie sat down at her desk and pulled the telephone closer. 'But since I can't spend my savings,' she added tartly, 'I'll have to get busy and sell another house.'

'Just don't count on it being Whiteoaks,' Tony warned.

Stephanie sighed. I didn't need him to tell me that, she thought. Caught between Jordan on the one hand and the unpredictable heirs on the other—No, Stephanie told herself, she wasn't counting on anything. Except trouble, of course. She could almost guarantee that there was more trouble coming her way.

The telephone was ringing when Stephanie struggled in through the back door with two big bags of groceries. So much for my peaceful Saturday morning, she thought. I can ignore the phone and hope it will go away, or I can run to answer it and probably miss it after all.

'Does it always take you this long to wake up?' Jordan asked politely when she answered.

Stephanie counted to ten. 'I was not asleep,' she said coldly. 'I was out. Did you call for a reason, or just to harrass me?'

'I'd like to have Katie for the day, if you don't mind.'

I mind, she thought. I mind very much indeed. She was marshalling her words for a refusal when she looked out the front window and caught a glimpse of Katie, in her orange jacket, pedalling her tricycle furiously up the pavement. But Katie would love it, she reminded herself. Another whole day with her daddy—she hadn't stopped talking about the last one, yet. Besides, if she said no, there was no telling what Jordan might do. 'Sure, Jordan,' she said finally, with resignation.

'I'll pick her up in an hour, then.' He didn't wait for an answer.

Stephanie put the telephone down with a sigh and went back to her groceries. Darn Jordan anyway, she thought. That hadn't been a request; it had been a demand—

And refusing him will get you nothing but trouble, she reminded herself. A father did have certain rights when it came to his child, and if Jordan chose to take the matter back to a judge, Stephanie would be stuck with regular visiting hours and days, and maybe worse than that. She knew that he was being perfectly reasonable, and that she had given the only answer she could. But it still felt as if she was being blackmailed.

Think positive, she told herself sternly. It meant that she and Tony could go to the auction in peace, and stay as long as they liked, without Katie's restless boredom. But the idea didn't make Stephanie feel better.

She was unpacking the bags of food when her father banged on the back door. 'Do you have a cup of coffee for a freezing man?' he begged.

'Did you walk all the way over?' Stephanie reached for a mug.

'A man has to get his exercise somehow,' Karl pointed out. 'I figure when I was working, I walked five miles a day on the production line. Now that I'm retired—' He patted his waistline ruefully. 'Your mother's cooking tends to build up.' He wrapped his hands around the mug and looked curiously over the array of food on the counter. 'Stocking up for the winter?'

Stephanie shook her head. 'Just replacing what Katie used to make pancakes the morning I was sick. Breakfast that morning cost me as much as it would to eat out for a week.'

'I heard a little about that,' Karl agreed. 'I'd have

been in earlier but I ran into her on the pavement and she wanted to chat.'

Stephanie, who was quite familiar with Katie's chats, nodded. 'The six o'clock news starring Katie?'

'Something like that.' Karl sipped his coffee and said, carefully, 'She was rattling on about Jordan.'

'That's not surprising.'

'Has he been seeing a lot of her?'

'He's taking her out for the day.'

Karl said, very calmly and without expression, a word that Stephanie had never heard him utter before. It shocked her.

'Dad!' she protested.

Karl shrugged. 'He hasn't shown a speck of interest in her in four years. Now all of a sudden he's hanging over her and she's tickled to death with the attention.'

'Dad—' she started to say. Oh, God, she thought, I have to clear this up. I've let it wait too long as it is.

'What happens to Katie when he gets tired of her, Steph? The only reason he's doing it is to annoy you —we both know that. But when he gets bored, it's Katie who will be hurt.' He set his cup down with a bang. 'The guy ought to be tarred and feathered, Stephanie, and I'm not going to sit around and watch while he hurts my granddaughter!'

'To say nothing of your daughter,' she put in mildly. 'Dad—there's something you should know.'

His eyes narrowed. 'If you're going to tell me that he's forced himself on you—'

'Heavens, no! Jordan hasn't touched me. At least—' Abruptly, those few dizzy moments in his arms, while he carried her across the house and put her into bed, flashed through her mind, and Stephanie's traitorous transparent skin flushed guiltily. She hurried on and hoped her father wouldn't notice. 'There's nothing he wants less than that, Dad.'

'What he did to you the first time around was bad enough,' Karl said. 'Leaving you alone like that, with a baby on the way, not caring enough to ask about Katie even once in all these years.'

She could stand it no longer. There would be no easy way to break it to him. 'He didn't know about Katie,' she blurted out. 'I never told him.'

There was a long silence.

'He isn't quite the bad guy you think,' she went on, quietly. 'I let you believe that, because I really think I hated him when I first came home. After that, there was no way to tell you—' Her voice trailed off.

'And now you're standing up for him.' Karl's voice was gentle.

'Of course I'm not! I just don't think it's fair to blame him when he didn't know—'

Katie burst in through the front door. 'Daddy's here! Daddy's here!'

'First chance I've had to give him a piece of my mind,' Karl mused. He sounded as if he was looking forward to it.

Stephanie started to protest, and then swallowed the words. Her father would not be stopped, no matter what she said. She could just as well try to stop rain from falling.

This is going to be awful, she thought.

She looked up at Jordan as he crossed the room towards her, Katie hanging on to his hand. His dark hair was windswept, and he was casually dressed, as though for a hike. No tie and sports coat, Stephanie thought idly. He was better prepared for Katie today.

His eyes flicked over her, assessing the slender curves under her trim-fitting jeans and sweater. A question flickered through her mind. I wonder what he thinks, when he looks at me.

But there was no warmth in his expression. He might as well have been looking at a plastic doll, she thought indignantly, instead of the woman he used to hold, and caress, and make love to.

And that train of thought, she told herself sternly, is a dangerous one. Physical passion is not a good basis for anything; the two of them were certainly a shining example of that. And to think about those long ago days when the passion held a promise of happiness was to court disaster and repeated heartbreak.

'Would you like coffee?' she asked. There was a breathless note in her voice that she would have given anything to avoid, but it was too late.

Jordan didn't seem to notice it. 'Sure,' he said, and immediately turned his attention to the man at the table. 'Karl,' he said, extending a hand. 'I'm glad to see you again.'

Stephanie saw her father's jaw clench. Then he said, civilly enough, 'I've been wanting to talk to you, Jordan.'

She handed Jordan his cup. He didn't look at her as he took it and sat down at the table across from Karl. 'That makes two of us,' he said. 'Jake McDonald says you're the best supervisor he's ever known. My question is, are you happily retired, or would you consider coming back to work?'

Katie was impatiently tugging at his arm. 'I'll be with you in a minute, Peanut,' he told her and set her on his knee. She snuggled her face into his shoulder.

Karl's face was a study. Stephanie, from her post in the kitchen doorway, wanted to burst out laughing at the war that was going on behind those tanned features. A muscle in his jaw twitched, and he opened his mouth a couple of times to respond, and then closed it again firmly. Stephanie wanted to applaud. A master stroke, Jordan, she thought.

'Not as a supervisor, though,' Jordan added, and sipped his coffee. 'What I really need is a personnel manager—someone who knows the people around here and who can hire wisely. Jake McDonald says you're it—but he didn't know if you wanted to go back to work.'

Karl was fast losing the battle, Stephanie could see. Much as he would like to throw Jordan's offer back in his teeth, the attraction of a new job, a new challenge, was too much for him.

Stephanie swallowed a smile as she watched him struggle. 'I don't know anything about robots,' he said.

'It doesn't matter. You'll be working with the people, anyway. We'll teach you what you need to know about the robots.'

'I've always wanted that kind of job,' Karl admitted.

'Good. Can you start next week? We won't be beginning production for a couple of months because of all the remodelling in the plant, but I'd like to start hiring right away.'

'Sure,' Karl said. He sounded a little dazed.

'Shouldn't you ask Mom what she thinks, first?' Stephanie asked. Anne's reaction might take a good deal of the humour out of the situation. Having Karl working for Jordan—Stephanie wasn't so sure she liked the idea after all.

'She won't mind.' Karl stood up, decisively. 'But I'd better walk home and tell her, anyway.'

Jordan drained his coffee cup. 'I'll give you a ride, if you like.'

Stephanie trailed them out to the car. 'Wait a minute,' she demanded. 'Jordan, I'd like to at least know where you're taking Katie today.'

'To the football game.'

'Football?' She sounded a little doubtful. 'You were never a football fan.'

He shrugged. 'I never had the time before. I'll have her home by bedtime.'

'I doubt she'll sit still for a whole game.'

'Don't you think that's my problem, not yours?' He

bent his head to check Katie's seatbelt.

Tony's car pulled into the driveway, and there was a sickening thud and the screech of metal.

He smashed the back of that beautiful Lincoln, Stephanie thought. I can't believe he did that—

But the Lincoln was unscratched. Tony got out of his car, slammed the door, and picked up Katie's tricycle from the drive. The front wheel was bent almost double, and Tony's face was red with fury as he flung the frame into the front lawn.

'I've told her a hundred times not to leave that damned thing in the driveway,' he scolded.

Katie craned her neck to see the destruction, and burst into tears. 'My trike!' she wailed at the top of her lungs.

If any of the neighbours are listening to the noise, Stephanie thought, they'll turn us all in for child abuse!

'Katie,' she said sternly. 'You know your tricycle is to be put away—'

'It seems to me,' Jordan said firmly, cutting across the noise of Katie's wails, 'that any competent driver should be able to see a tricycle at high noon in a driveway.'

'What that kid needs,' Tony raved, 'is some firm discipline from a father, for a change!'

Jordan lifted an eyebrow. 'I couldn't agree with you more,' he said. His voice was cordial, but there was an edge to it as he continued, 'But since you're not her father, butt out. Keep your hands, and your vicious tongue, off my daughter. Now if you will move your car, I'll be happy to take myself and Katie out of your hair for the day.'

Stephanie, unwilling to take sides in this quarrel, retreated to the house. When Tony came in a little later, she was putting the last of her groceries away.

'Tyrannical so-and-so, isn't he?' Tony said. 'How did you manage to put up with him?'

Stephanie shrugged. 'I never thought about it.'

'Well, you were young. You probably didn't know any better,' Tony concluded. 'Though it was a bit foolish of you not to wait a while to get married. It would have saved a heck of a lot of trouble for everyone.'

Did he include Katie in his definition of trouble? Stephanie decided not to pursue that question. 'Let's not waste a precious day in quarrelling about Jordan,' she said. She reached up to put a box of cereal into a high cabinet.

Tony came up behind her. He put his arms around her waist and buried his face in her hair. 'That's right,' he said unsteadily. 'Why waste time on him, when it's just us today? Let's skip the auction and stay home—have a little fun this afternoon.' His hands slid up from her narrow waist to cup her breasts.

She was mildly amused that the auction that had been so important earlier now had lost all appeal for him. It was nice to know, she thought, that she was still attractive to a man . . .

Tony pulled her back against him. 'Katie's always in the way,' he complained. 'She's always sitting between us, or fussing for your attention. Now that we have a free afternoon, we can spend it by ourselves. I want you so badly, Stephanie—' His mouth was hot against the side of her throat. 'Please, darling—'

And why not, she thought. This was the man she was going to marry, the man with whom she would spend the rest of her life. What could be wrong with anticipating the wedding night? She was just a little flattered, too. Tony had always been willing to wait till they were married. He had never acted like this, like an impatient lover . . . Sometimes his very patience had irritated her, made her wonder if he found her physically attractive at all.

She turned in his arms, warm and willing, and raised her face for his kiss. It had been so long, she thought, since she had felt the flames of passion.

His mouth was hesitant at first, and then as she remained passive, it became plundering, almost bruising her lips with its intensity. Eyes closed, Stephanie waited for that remembered fire to flicker over her again.

But it didn't come. She tried to will it into existence, but it was as if Jordan was standing in the corner of the kitchen, arms folded, eyebrows raised, watching with amusement.

Go away, she begged him silently. You've tormented me for all these years. Leave me alone now.

But the image conjured by her own memories remained, and finally she twisted out of Tony's arms with a moan.

'What's the matter, darling?' he asked solicitously.

'I can't,' she muttered, grasping for an excuse he would accept. 'It's a bad example for Katie.'

There was a long silent moment. 'But Katie isn't here,' Tony pointed out.

'I—I think it's better to wait,' she said, a little wildly. 'I want to be honest with her, and if we were to sleep together before we're married—well, I couldn't be truthful.'

He sighed heavily. 'It's always Katie, isn't it?' he asked. 'I guess there's no point in talking about it any more.' He reached for his jacket. 'Let's go to the auction.'

She swallowed hard, thankful that he wasn't going to press the matter. What she had done was unforgivable, that she knew.

Go away, Jordan, she begged inside. All we had was that physical bond, and it wasn't enough. So let me go now. Let me be free of you. Let me love Tony as I want to love him . . .

She knew, deep in her heart, that unless she could wipe the memory of Jordan from her mind, there would be no peace. But she knew of no way to exorcise the ghost that haunted her.

CHAPTER SEVEN

It was late when they left the auction. The air was chilly, and the damp seemed to cut through her coat. Stephanie couldn't help murmuring, as she relaxed in the warmth of the car, 'I hope Katie isn't cold. All she was wearing was a light jacket, and if she's been sitting all day at a football game—'

'She won't freeze, Stephanie.' Tony sounded irritable. 'Do you realise how many times you've brought her into the conversation today? For heaven's sake, Katie isn't even here, and you still can't leave her out of it!'

'I'm sorry, Tony.' She fell silent, remembering how right he was. But she couldn't help worrying about the child. Jordan didn't know Katie very well, after all, and he didn't have a mother's instinct to warn him what to do.

'Would you like to come in?' she asked.

Tony shook his head, and Stephanie couldn't help feeling a little relieved. She knew that she had brought most of the problems on to herself, by leading him on and then refusing him. That, plus the accident with Katie's tricycle, had doomed the day. But after hours of Tony's brooding, Stephanie was ready for a little peaceful silence.

'I'll see you Monday, then,' she said.

He didn't even wait for her to reach the door before he revved the engine and backed out of the drive. Sometimes, Stephanie thought, I get so furious with him that I just want him to go away forever—

The thought struck her with the force of a hammer. No, I don't, she told herself. Of course I get irritated.

We all get angry sometimes with people we love. I get angry with Katie, too, but it doesn't mean that I don't want her any more!

Today had been a difficult one, though. Every time she had slipped and mentioned Katie's name, Tony had had a comment about her bad manners, her carelessness, her tomboyishness. Stephanie had wanted to scream, more than once, 'She is a child, for heaven's sake! What do you expect her to be, Miss America at the age of four?'

But she had bitten her tongue, because she knew that Tony didn't really mean most of it the way it sounded. Besides, it was all true. Katie was a tomboy, and she was careless, and she frequently displayed the worst manners Stephanie had ever seen, always when Tony was around.

Of course Tony isn't always pleased with her behaviour, Stephanie thought. Sometimes even I don't want to claim her, and I'm her mother. We're going to work on those manners, starting tonight.

The fresh air had left her ravenous, and she searched the cupboards. 'Wouldn't you think,' she asked, her voice echoing in the empty house, 'that since I just stocked the kitchen this morning, there would be something I want to eat?'

She decided to settle for scrambled eggs and toast, and put the skillet on. She reached for the necessary tools, and caught the drawer with the skill of long practice as it dropped awkwardly forward. It had been broken for weeks, and she kept forgetting to ask her father to fix it. It was one of the aggravations of being a non-mechanical woman, living alone.

She put the butter in the skillet and cracked an egg into a cup. 'I wonder when they'll be home,' she murmured. She hadn't expected that it would be this late. She couldn't imagine sitting through a whole football game with Katie. Either Jordan had the patience of a saint or he was a plain fool . . .

And in either case, how long would it last? Was her father right, that Jordan was paying so much attention to Katie just because he knew it irritated Stephanie? And if that was so, how long would it be before the visits and the special days together stopped, and Jordan found more important things to do? Katie would be devastated . . .

The front door banged, and she heard Katie's excited chatter.

It must have been a good day, she thought idly, listening to Katie's bubbly laugh and the deep, quiet note of Jordan's voice in reply. 'Not just yet, Katie,' he was saying.

You will be polite, and pleasant, she told herself. You will not show irritation, or curiosity, or anger—

She stepped into the dining room, a smile carefully planted on her lips, and said, 'How was the game?'

Katie danced across the room to her. 'See my new coat, Mommy? Daddy bought it for me!'

Stephanie's smile froze. Katie twirled in front of her, and the hood fell back from an excited little face. Katie's dark hair had slipped from pigtails to fall over the soft white fur.

'Why did you buy a four-year-old a white fur coat?' she asked, her voice taut.

'Because she was cold. We did come back to the house for a sweater, but the doors were locked, so we went shopping instead.'

Stephanie had a momentary vision of what would have happened if she and Tony had not gone to the auction after all. To have Katie—and Jordan—show up on the doorstep unexpectedly would have been a nightmare come true.

But it didn't happen, she told herself crossly, so stop thinking about it!

'Katie thought it was the prettiest one in the store,'

Jordan went on calmly. 'It was, too.' He tossed his own jacket across a chair.

'White?' Stephanie's voice was rising.

'It's washable,' Jordan pointed out. 'It's only fake fur, after all.'

'I didn't mistake it for ermine, thank you! But a white fur coat for a child who—'

Jordan shushed her with a finger to his lips, then pointed down at Katie. Wide-eyed, she was absorbing the exchange, and her face had started to crumple into tears.

The damage is done, Stephanie told herself. If he wants to waste his money on white fur coats, there is no point in making Katie miserable. 'It's a lovely coat, darling,' she told the child, kneeling beside her and brushing a hand across the fur trim.

'It's a princess coat,' Katie confided, her face clearing. 'The lady said so.'

Stephanie had to laugh. 'She meant that's what the style is called, Katie. But you do look like a princess in it.'

Katie unbuttoned the coat. 'And a new sweater, and new jeans, and new shoes—' She held up a foot to show off a brand-name running shoe.

'I didn't know they made those things that small,' Stephanie said tightly. She didn't look up at Jordan. If she had, she would have screamed at him to leave them alone, that she was perfectly capable of keeping her daughter clothed . . .

'Neither did I,' he said comfortably. 'It was a great deal of fun.'

'I'll just bet it was. I'm amazed that you had time for the football game.'

'We didn't, actually. The first half was dull, and Katie was getting cold, so—'

'So you went shopping instead. I see. Katie, go hang up your coat now, and get cleaned up for supper.'

'Not hungry,' Katie announced.

'She ate all afternoon,' Jordan said. 'I'll take the blame for that. Two hot dogs and an ice cream sundae and a pickle on a stick and a frozen banana—'

'And are you going to stay up with her when she has a stomach ache tonight?' Stephanie snapped.

'I'd love to.' For an instant their gazes met and locked. Then Jordan went on, his voice even and hard, 'But I was never given the opportunity to take part in raising my daughter. You kept that right all for yourself.'

Stephanie's eyes fell.

'And before you get on the high ropes about the new clothes, Stephanie,' he went on, with an angry edge to his voice, 'if I was trying to show you up as a bad parent, I'd have bought her a whole wardrobe. This was just a late birthday present, so don't go getting offended at it.'

'Mommy,' Katie said.

'Don't interrupt, Kathleen,' Stephanie told her. 'I suppose you think, Jordan, that coming back into our lives now means that you have all sorts of rights where Katie is concerned—'

'Mommy,' Katie said plaintively.

'Be careful, Stephanie,' he warned, very quietly. 'Don't push me. And while we're on the subject, let's get one thing clear. I haven't come back into your life. I don't give a damn about you. But I'll go to hell and back for Katie.'

'You are not going to take this child away from me.' Despite her efforts, there was a tremor in Stephanie's voice. 'You can't. I'm not an unfit parent. There is nothing you can use against me—'

'But there is, my dear,' he said. He sounded a little surprised. 'You might have some trouble explaining your strange oversight to a judge. The mere fact that you never told me that Katie existed—'

'I had no reason to think you'd be interested.' Stephanie's voice was hoarse.

'Mommy!' Katie was tugging on her arm.

Jordan looked down at the child, and then back at Stephanie. 'I think Kathleen wants to talk to you about the smoke that is seeping in here from the kitchen.'

'Oh, my God!' Stephanie ran for the stove. The butter that she had intended to scramble her egg in had turned ugly black and was sending clouds of smoke through the kitchen. She reached for a holder to move the skillet, which was hot as a blast furnace, and swore as the drawer dropped forward on to her hand.

'What's the matter with the drawer?' Jordan had followed her to the kitchen.

'It's broken, what did you think the problem was?' Stephanie set the hot skillet in the sink, where it sizzled ominously.

He slanted a look at her and worked the drawer out of the cabinet so he could get a good look at it.

Stephanie flung a window open and snapped, 'I don't need your assistance, Jordan. I am not completely help-less.'

He looked up with the first honest amusement she had seen on his face since he had arrived in town. 'Oh, yeah?' he drawled. 'I will always remember the day you put up bookshelves in the living room of our apartment.'

Stephanie remembered it too. 'At least I tried,' she said defensively.

Jordan stopped whistling and said thoughtfully, 'And I will never forget the next day, when we had to replaster the wall after the screws pulled loose and dumped the whole works on to the floor.'

'How was I to know that the brackets only went into the plaster? They seemed solid enough to hold the weight of a few books.'

'And the shelves were even almost level,' Jordan agreed. He inspected the back of the drawer. 'The guide wheel has come loose. Simple enough to fix. Do you have a Phillips screwdriver?'

Unwilling to admit that she wasn't certain which kind that was, Stephanie pointed to the bottom drawer. She poured a little water into the still-hot skillet, and a cloud of steam rose furiously.

'Tell me about Mommy,' Katie demanded. She was standing beside Jordan, her thumb in her mouth.

'Some other time, Peanut. We couldn't even get a fair start tonight.' He tightened the last screw and replaced the drawer, testing its now smooth motion. 'All fixed.' He raised an eyebrow enquiringly.

Stephanie bit her tongue and then said, reluctantly, 'Thanks, Jordan.'

'A little ungracious, but better than nothing,' he mused. Then, softly, 'Steph, I'm sorry I offended you with the clothes. I should have asked, but I honestly didn't think it would make any difference.'

She was surprised, both by the tone of his voice and the softness of his words. It felt so strange, to have Jordan apologise . . .

'I guess I'm not really upset,' she said finally. 'Goodness knows she needs the things. It just took me by surprise. And the white coat—really, Jordan, what a foolish thing to buy for a child!'

'When I was a kid,' he mused, 'I would have given anything to have had a wool sports jacket. Cream-coloured wool—they had one in the store window, and I used to stand there with my nose pressed against the glass and look at it. My mother said it wasn't practical, so I never got it.'

For a moment, Stephanie thought she was imagining his words. She held her breath, afraid that any movement might shatter the confiding moment. Jordan had never talked to her like this before.

'I resented her for a long time,' he said thoughtfully, 'even after she died, because I knew I would have taken good care of it, but she wouldn't give me a chance to prove it. It wasn't until I was almost grown that I realised she had said no because she couldn't afford it.'

Tears were misting in Stephanie's eyes. She had known that Jordan's family had been poor, but he had always behaved as if it made no difference.

'I almost told Katie today that the white coat wasn't sensible,' he said, 'and then I remembered my jacket.'

She put a hand out, blindly. He took it, and they stood there for a brief moment, the warmth of their fingers like a kind of cement that bound them together.

Stephanie let her fingers slide out of his, feeling a little silly at her own sentimentality. For all she knew it was only a story, told to soften her up. If that had been his intention, he had certainly succeeded.

'Weren't you going to have supper?' he asked.

She shook her head. 'I'm not hungry any more.' She led the way back to the living room, wishing that he would go away, but knowing better than to ask him to leave.

Katie had flung herself down on the carpet with her woolly blanket, and Jordan joined her there, stretching out comfortably. 'All the comforts of home,' he murmured.

Stephanie looked at him with a jaundiced eye. 'It's hardly as elegant as what you're used to,' she pointed out. 'But there's something to be said for casual.'

'Just what do you think I'm used to?' he asked, his eyes closed. 'What are you finding out about Whiteoaks?'

'I wouldn't start packing just yet. Why are you so anxious?'

'Because I'm living in a hotel room. It's enough to make a man cry.'

'Oh. I thought you were staying with the McDonalds.'

He opened his eyes. 'I was invited. Hallie adores me.'

'I can't see why. You'd be a miserable houseguest —always coming and going at odd hours, never in for meals—But perhaps you should brush up the friendship.

Hallie is one of the owners of Whiteoaks.' Then she sat back and waited for his face to show astonishment.

He didn't oblige. 'If you expect me to be surprised, think again. Surely you don't believe I'd leave something as important as Whiteoaks entirely up to you?'

'I'm touched by your trust in me,' Stephanie snapped.

'So what have you found out?' he countered.

'Correct me wherever I'm wrong,' she said cattily. 'You're out of luck, Jordan. They can't agree on anything, certainly not when it comes to selling it.' Then she relented. 'I haven't talked to Hallie directly. I thought that would be a good job for you. Beth Anderson wants to sell. In fact, she's desperate for cash, and if Whiteoaks would sell she won't have to get rid of her own house.'

'You're cheating yourself out of a commission there, Stephanie.'

'Not really. Tony listed the Anderson house—I only benefit if I'm the one who makes the sale.'

'Somehow I would have expected that,' Jordan muttered.

Stephanie pretended not to have heard. 'I'm not certain about the other two heirs, but, from what Beth says, they would be happy to get rid of the headache. Hallie seems to be the one who is holding back. In fact, a couple of years ago she tried to get the others to sell it to the local historical society.'

Jordan shook his head. 'This isn't making sense. I thought you said she didn't want to sell it.'

'For one dollar. It would have been a donation, actually, with fantastic tax advantages for the Mc-Donalds, even if it wouldn't have been so nice for the other owners. Hallie wants the society to turn Whiteoaks into a museum, and she wanted to be certain they had plenty of time to raise the necessary money.'

'It takes that long to raise a dollar around here?' Jordan mused.

'Don't be silly. It would take thousands to convert it, and then they aren't sure they can pay the heating bills in winter.'

'But the other heirs didn't feel like making a donation to the historical society.'

'Right. The society can't afford to buy the three of them out; Hallie refuses to sell to anyone else, and Whiteoaks is standing there mouldering away.'

'Maybe I'd better start looking for an apartment,' Jordan mused.

'Why not a different house? Be reasonable, Jordan. Whiteoaks is out of reach.'

'I want to look at it anyway,' he said.

Stephanie sighed. 'All right. I'll ask Beth Anderson for her key. Then will you be reasonable?'

'That depends on what you mean by reasonable,' he said. 'Are you willing to make a small wager on it?'

'On what?'

'Whether I'm living in Whiteoaks by Christmas.'

'I don't gamble.'

'How about double or nothing on your commission?'

'No, thanks. I probably won't earn one anyway, no matter what you buy.'

'That's the best odds I can give you. Christmas is only two months away.'

'I don't trust you, no matter what the odds are.'

'Christmas?' Katie repeated.

'Now you've done it,' Stephanie grumbled. 'I'll be hearing about Santa Claus for the next two solid months.'

'Sorry. It's probably wise not to bet against me,' Jordan agreed. 'I do have an ace or two up my sleeve.'

Katie looked puzzled. 'What's in your sleeve, Daddy?' she asked, and put her little hand on his arm.

'Same thing that's in yours, Peanut. An arm.' Jordan ran a finger up under Katie's sweater sleeve, and she giggled.

'That tickles, Daddy.' Then her eyes sparkled and she retaliated, and in two minutes she was helpless on the floor, being held down and gently tickled.

'Mommy!' she shrieked between her giggles. 'Help me!'

'That is hardly fair competition, Jordan,' Stephanie pointed out. 'Katie, Daddy's neck is ticklish.'

'No coaching from the sidelines,' Jordan threatened.

Stephanie raised an eyebrow. 'Oh? What are you going to do about it? Blow in his ear, Katie.'

Moments later, an iron grip clenched Stephanie's ankle and dragged her off the couch. Katie, with her father's attention distracted, wriggled free.

It had been years since Stephanie had engaged in such childish horseplay with anyone but Katie, and it was only moments before she found herself winded and helpless, pinned down by the length of Jordan's body, his long fingers counting her ribs as she squirmed. Then, in the space of a breath, she knew that it was horseplay no longer.

'You smell like baby powder,' Jordan said, with a catch in his voice as if he didn't understand what was happening.

'I ran out of my usual stuff, so I borrowed Katie's.' Stephanie didn't even know what she was saying. She was aware only of his dark eyes, of the tanned face close to hers, of the warmth of his body seeming to scorch her skin. 'I can't breathe,' she whispered.

And then, it seemed, there was no need for breath, for her body was taking its sustenance from his. Their mouths strained together. She remembered the taste of him as if their last kiss had been but yesterday. She was only vaguely aware of his arousal, but painfully so of hers. The fire in the pit of her stomach ached to be quenched as only he could quench it.

His hand slipped slowly from her ribs up to her breast, and Stephanie sighed, deep in her throat. She was incapable of coherent thought; she could remember only the wild joy of his possession. Nothing else mattered, nothing else was real, but the pressure of his body against hers.

Katie said plaintively, 'Mommy. Daddy. Play with me!'

My God, Stephanie thought. I forgot that Katie was even here . . . She looked up into Jordan's eyes, dark with a passion she remembered well. 'Why have you come here?' she whispered. It was only a breath. 'Leave me alone, Jordan. Let me go.'

She watched as sanity dawned in his eyes, and felt the cold trickle of reality returning to her own body, still pinned to the carpet by his weight. Then he rolled away from her and on to his back, one forearm across his eyes as if he didn't want to see her or comprehend what he had almost done.

Katie chuckled and flung herself on him again, and Stephanie took advantage of the opportunity to scramble to her feet, straightening her hair by raking trembling fingers through it.

'It's bedtime, Katie,' she said, hoping that Jordan would take the hint to leave. But he didn't seem to hear. He was still lying there when she took a grumbling Katie off for her bath.

'I want Daddy,' Katie told her as Stephanie helped her into her pyjamas and combed her silky hair up into a ponytail. 'I want Daddy to read my story and hear my prayers.'

Stephanie was too tired to fight it. 'Very well, Katie.' She started for the door.

'And you, too, Mommy.'

Jordan was staring out the front window, his hands deep in his pockets, a frown cutting deep lines into his face. He turned as Stephanie came into the room, but the frown didn't ease.

He doesn't even want to look at me, she thought. It's a

funny thing, how two people can be so damned compatible in the bedroom, and not even like each other outside it. 'The princess is ready to be tucked in,' she said.

Katie was yawning by the time Jordan had finished reading her story. Stephanie, sitting in the rocker beside Katie's bed, was doing her best not to listen, but she couldn't help but hear that gorgeous baritone of his, unselfconscious, seeming to enjoy the simple story.

Then Katie said, 'Daddy, can we ask Mommy now about my bicycle?'

'What bicycle?' Stephanie asked, with foreboding.

'Daddy says—'

'Katie,' her father put in quickly, 'I think you've done enough damage for one evening. We'll talk about it next time, all right?'

'All right,' Katie said reluctantly, and yawned again, snuggled her woolly blanket around her shoulders, and settled down to sleep.

Stephanie paused outside the room. 'Just a minute. What bicycle?'

'There's a baby bike downtown,' Jordan admitted. 'It's no bigger than her tricycle, and it has training wheels. We thought—'

'No.' All the pent-up frustration of the evening rushed back to her, and her voice began to rise. 'Stop trying to buy her away from me, Jordan. I'm her mother—I'll provide for her!' She was so furious that tears were starting to blur her vision. 'And just because she wants you to tuck her in, it doesn't mean that she'd rather live with you! You're a new toy as far as she's concerned —you're like a big live teddy bear!'

He had never looked less like a toy. He looked big, and angry, and on the verge of violence. 'Are you finished, Stephanie?' he said, and his voice was deceptively level.

'Not quite.' She pushed her hair back out of her eyes, held her chin up defiantly, and said, 'Leave us alone,

Jordan. We don't want you. We don't need you. Just go away and let us forget about you.'

He picked up his jacket. At the door, he turned, and said, almost gently, 'Don't kid yourself. You haven't forgotten, Stephanie. And you never will.'

CHAPTER EIGHT

IT was raining, a dingy, dull autumn rain, and Stephanie felt just about as gloomy as the weather outside. To be perfectly honest, she admitted, a great deal of her gloom had to do with the polished brass key that lay atop her desk blotter. It was the key to Whiteoaks, and she knew that she had to call Jordan today and show him the house. She could not postpone the matter any longer.

She hadn't seen him since the night he had stalked out of her house, three days before. She had long been sleepless that night, thinking about the explosive embrace on the living room floor, blaming herself, going over and over in her mind what she could have done to avoid it, what she should do in the future.

If Katie hadn't been in the room, she knew, they might well have forgotten all but their physical longings. Stephanie herself had been close enough, she admitted, cheeks burning in the darkened bedroom. All that had mattered to her in those mad moments had been the demands of their bodies, the overpowering desire to be one.

It frightened her. Was she some kind of sex maniac, that she could respond that way to a man she didn't even like?

Yet there had been a few moments that evening when she had glimpsed a Jordan she hardly recognised. When he was with Katie, he was gentle, patient, warm—different than she had ever suspected him to be. Which man was he?

Then she had drawn herself up short in her speculations. What sort of person Jordan was had nothing to do with it, she told herself sternly. The fact was, she was

engaged to one man and had allowed herself a passionate wrestling match in the middle of the living room
floor with another. That was the only fact that mattered.

Besides, she reminded herself crossly, Jordan had
been just as upset at what had happened as she had been.
The flare of passion between them had surprised him
just as it had her, and been just as unwelcome. As for
future trouble, there wouldn't be any, she told herself
firmly. Jordan was no more interested in a repeat per-
formance than she was.

But in the three days since, she hadn't seen him. He
hadn't called, and though Katie had asked a few times
about him, she didn't seem to miss him.

Maybe, Stephanie thought, he is doing what I asked
—leaving us alone. Maybe he's tired of the game.
Maybe he's frightened that I was so delighted at his
attentions that I'll beg him to take me back . . .

He needn't worry about that, she mused. I have
not the least desire to live with Jordan Kendall ever
again.

She leafed through her appointment book and found
the phone number for the factory. His voice was curt
when he came to the telephone.

'I have the key to Whiteoaks,' she said.

There was a brief silence.

Maybe he doesn't want to see me any more than I
want to see him, she thought. 'If you'd like, I can ask
Tony to show you through it this afternoon.'

'Why Tony?'

'Or Susan. I think she's free today.'

'Why not you, Stephanie? Are you backing out of our
deal? Tony might not be pleased at the idea of losing all
those commissions when the rest of my people come to
town.'

'Tony is foolish enough to believe that you'll really
come through with them,' she snapped. 'I'm not. Shall I
meet you at the house?'

'Pick me up at the factory, instead. My car is being worked on.'

'That's what happens when you buy new,' Stephanie said sweetly. 'You have to work the bugs out yourself.'

There was a split second of silence, and then he struck back. 'Besides, I don't have time to waste in waiting for you today.'

Stephanie was incensed. 'I have never kept a client waiting in my life!'

'Then I recommend that you don't start today.' He didn't give her a chance to answer.

She put the phone down with a bang and flung her appointment book across the room. It bounced off the wall and skidded back towards her, loose pages fluttering across the floor. Instantly her anger died as she realised the trouble she had caused herself now, and she bent to pick up the mess.

Tony came to the door of his office just then. He was shaking his head sadly. 'Stephanie, when will you learn to control that temper? It's no wonder that Katie throws tantrums when she sees you do it, too.'

Stephanie gritted her teeth to keep from throwing the book at him.

'What are you so mad at, anyway?' He reached for the business section of the morning paper.

'Jordan, what else? I'm taking him to see Whiteoaks this afternoon.'

Tony raised his head from the tiny print in the stock market report. 'I thought he had given up on that nonsense.'

'Jordan never gives up on anything.' She didn't really hear the words till after they were said, and then a superstitious little shiver ran down her spine. He won't give up on Katie, either, she thought. He hasn't gone out of her life. He's plotting something, and I'm not going to like it one bit.

But there was no sense in worrying until she knew in

which direction the danger lay, she told herself sternly. Trying to read Jordan Kendall's mind was hopeless.

The McDonald plant—it was the Robonics plant now, Stephanie reminded herself—lay on the edge of town, sprawling across what had once been a cornfield. The factory had been only a few years old when Jake McDonald's manufacturing business had failed, a victim of changing needs in local agriculture.

She parked her little car in the employee lot. There were a surprising number of cars there, she thought, for a plant that wasn't yet open. But acres more lay empty, a reminder of the huge payroll that had helped to keep the little town solvent when Jake McDonald owned the factory. Would the parking lot ever be full again, she wondered.

There was no doubt that the building had been a good buy for Jordan, Stephanie knew. But she couldn't stop herself from cursing the luck that had brought him here, to her home town. And she knew that, no matter how much she wanted him to leave town, he was there to stay.

'At least until his business fails,' she told herself curtly. Sometimes it looked like her only hope.

A woman looked up from a desk in the front office as Stephanie came in. She was probably in her early thirties, and she was elegantly dressed in a style that wouldn't find its way to this little town for a year, at least. Quite a receptionist, Stephanie thought, and wondered what had brought her here. Surely company orders and a receptionist's pay would not be enough. Was it loyalty to Jordan that had taken her from the city—

You are being utterly ridiculous, Stephanie told herself crossly. The woman's motives are none of your concern. You don't even know that she's moved here, and why should you care? As for the rest, even if Jordan was to have an affair with her, it is none of your business.

'May I help you?' the woman said, and Stephanie

realised in embarrassment that it was not the first time she had been asked.

'Well, what gives us the pleasure of your company today?' Karl Daniels had come quietly out of an office with a stack of papers.

'Oh,' the woman said. 'If you're applying for a job, Miss—' She pushed a form across the desk with one finger.

Karl frowned. 'This is my daughter, Stephanie,' he said gently. 'Come in, dear—if you have a moment?'

'I'm waiting for Jordan.' Stephanie could see recognition dawning in the woman's eyes as she added up the score. 'Please tell him I'm here,' she told the woman gently.

'Of course, Mrs Kendall.' The tone had changed abruptly, Stephanie noted.

It answered one question, Stephanie told herself. The woman might have her eye on Jordan, but he obviously hadn't given her the details, or she would not have been frightened to meet Stephanie. She felt just a little better, and then started to scold herself. What difference could it possibly make to her, whatever Jordan did? So long as he left her alone, and Katie, he could do whatever else he darned well pleased.

She followed Karl into his office. 'Your receptionist needs a course in manners,' she said.

He grinned. 'You noticed? She isn't a receptionist, you know. She's one of the smartest computer programmers in the country.'

'Oh.' Stephanie wished that she'd looked the woman over more closely. Then she shrugged it off. What difference could it possibly make to her? 'How is the job going?' she asked. 'You look pretty sharp in that new suit.'

'It's different, Stephanie. No doubt about that. But I like it.' He waved her to a chair. 'Ask Jordan for a tour of the plant,' he suggested. 'I'd take you through myself, but I don't understand it well enough to be helpful.'

That's interesting, Stephanie thought. The note of respect in his voice came as a bit of a shock to her.

Karl saw her uplifted eyebrows, and said, thoughtfully, 'You know, when I first met Jordan I thought he was a smart kid—but one who thought he knew a lot more than he did. Even when I came out here to work, I expected him to be a stuffed shirt. The idea man, maybe, but too uppity to get his hands greasy. Well, I was wrong—'

'Please, Dad,' she said wearily. 'Spare me the list of Jordan's good qualities.'

'He's a hell of an engineer, Steph. And yet he can talk to anyone about anything. Seeing him with Katie is a real boost.'

'Oh?' What he had said was innocent enough, but there was a twinge of warning in the back of Stephanie's mind.

Karl laughed. 'You should have seen them yesterday wrestling with that darned pumpkin. Since Katie didn't have a big Jack-o-Lantern at Hallowe'en—'

'Pumpkin?' she said warily. Katie had said nothing about a pumpkin, much less anything about Jordan, last night.

Karl looked puzzled, and then understanding dawned in his eyes. 'Well, it doesn't matter,' he said.

'No, Dad. I think you'd better tell me about the pumpkin.'

He seized the opportunity. 'Biggest pumpkin I ever saw. Two hundred pounds, I think he said. They carved a face in it and—'

Stephanie cut in ruthlessly. 'Has Jordan been seeing Katie behind my back?'

He stammered a little. 'Well, I don't know about it being behind your back. I assumed Katie had told you all about it.'

'For once,' she said bitterly, 'my little darling seems to have known when to shut up. And you and Mom have been encouraging it.'

'Stephanie, what harm can it do? So he brought her a pumpkin. Big deal.'

'You're the one who warned me that Jordan would surely get tired of playing this game, and that Katie is the one who will suffer. And then you allow him—'

'Nobody allows me to do much of anything,' a voice from the door said. 'I do as I please.'

'Yes, I know,' Stephanie said bitterly. 'You always have, regardless of who got hurt. Well, it isn't going to be Katie who suffers for this, Jordan. I won't allow you to hurt her.'

'If anyone hurts Katie, it certainly won't be me. You're the one who tried to forbid me to see her. I simply exercised my rights as a parent, Stephanie.'

'And told her to keep it secret from me!'

He shook his head. 'I did nothing of the sort. Shall we stop inflicting our quarrel on your father?' He held the door open, and those brilliant blue eyes commanded her to walk out of the room.

That wasn't too smart, Stephanie berated herself. Getting involved in a fight of that sort with Dad looking on . . . It wouldn't make his job easier, to have the struggle over Katie dragged into it.

She couldn't even keep the flicker of anger at her father burning. After all, she hadn't told him not to let Jordan come near Katie. What was so wrong about him bringing her a pumpkin to carve?

'How big is a two hundred pound pumpkin, anyway?' she asked.

Jordan looked at her quizzically, and for a moment she was afraid that he would not accept the peace offering. Then he held out his arms in a circle. 'It's almost three feet across,' he said.

'In that case, I suppose I should say thank you for not

bringing it to my house,' Stephanie said quietly.

There was a moment of silence, and then he started to grin. 'Your mother did look a little less than enthusiastic about it,' he admitted.

The mere thought brought a twinkle to his eyes and erased the worry lines between his brows. It was an infectious grin, and Stephanie found herself smiling back, wishing that it could be like this between them all the time.

Then she drew herself up short. They had to deal together because of Katie, but that didn't mean that they had to be friends. She didn't want to be on that kind of terms with him; Jordan would not make a very comfortable kind of friend.

She let it drop there, knowing uneasily that if she had been pressed to explain her reasoning, she couldn't have done it. But she was certain that she didn't want to be his friend.

The rain had stopped, but as they drove by the battered, sagging front gate, Whiteoaks looked just about as dingy as it was possible for a house to look. It depressed Stephanie just to see the puddles standing in the driveway, the straggly weeds battered down by the pressure of the water, the tiles slickly wet—

'One good thing about it,' she said. 'We'll certainly be able to tell if the roof leaks.'

He flashed that smile again, and she felt her heart turn over. 'And if the basement is dry,' he agreed cheerfully.

It was cold inside, the bitter cold of a house that has been years without warmth. But it was more than central heating that was lacking, Stephanie thought as she stepped through the heavy, carved front door and into the long marble-floored hallway. It was the bone-chilling cold of loneliness that she felt. This was a house that was meant to shelter a family, and the cold had seeped into the walls as the seasons passed and it stood here empty and useless.

She shivered. 'You'd never get this house warmed up,' she said, but Jordan didn't hear. He had taken one appraising glance around the hall, and then turned as if by instinct to the left. Stephanie followed, hoping that it didn't take too long for him to get Whiteoaks out of his system. She wished that she had brought along a warmer coat.

The kitchen was a genuine antique. 'This is the only part they won't have to remodel for the museum,' she muttered.

Jordan looked up quizzically. 'What kind of salesman are you, anyway? You're supposed to be telling me that of course it's a bit dated, but tremendous things can be done for a few thousand dollars.'

'Quite a few thousand, I'd say,' Stephanie added. 'You'd have to strip it down to the bare walls.'

'Of course,' he said, as if there had never been any doubt in his mind. 'It was built for servants. You don't think the original owners ever set foot in this room, do you?'

Stephanie had wandered on. 'Now this is all right,' she said. 'A butler's pantry—what a wonderful idea. Why don't they build them in modern houses?'

Jordan had followed her, and she could feel the warmth that radiated from his body as he stood close behind her. Stephanie was torn; part of her wanted to move away, and another part wanted to snuggle up to the source of so much heat.

'Because no one has a butler any more,' he pointed out.

'I don't care. It would be wonderful to have all this shelf space just a step away from the kitchen, without having to walk around the stuff all the time.'

'A much better sales pitch,' he applauded. 'You'll get it all worked out in time.'

Reluctantly, she stepped away from him and went on through to the dining room. A big bay window looked out over the remains of a formal garden. It was almost choked with ivy and rose-bushes gone wild. 'You'd need a team of archaeologists to find out what's out there.'

Jordan shrugged and carefully opened the curved-glass door of a china cabinet built into the wall. 'These people didn't go second class, did they?' he asked, running a finger over the delicate leading that held the geometric shapes of glass together.

'Except, of course, where the servants were concerned,' Stephanie murmured. She stopped in the hall to poke about in the cupboards. For the most part, the house was empty, though here and there a piece of furniture had been left. Too big for regular houses, she diagnosed, or not to anyone's taste. With four heirs to the property, it must have been difficult for them to decide on anything.

Jordan had gone on, so she brushed the accumulated dust off her fingertips and followed. He seemed to know his way around almost by instinct, she thought. So far, she hadn't seen anything that impressed her much. Jordan hadn't made any of the standard comments that usually allowed her to gauge the interest a client had in a particular house. Not that the lack of response was any surprise with Jordan, she reflected.

The low, narrow hall opened out suddenly before her into a huge, high-ceilinged drawing room, and just as she stepped in, the sun peeked from behind a cloud. Beams of light trickled through the diamond-shaped panes in the casement windows and shattered into rainbows that chased each other about the room.

Stephanie uttered an uncontrollable little cry at the sheer beauty of the room, and in that instant she saw why Jordan had fallen in love with Whiteoaks.

The light, the charm, the magic, the music—they're all still here, she thought. They're just frozen—locked up till someone comes to thaw them out again.

Jordan had been inspecting the fireplace, and he

banged his head against the mantel when she called out. He emerged, rubbing the bump, but it took only an instant for him to see what had caused the exclamation. 'The house kind of reaches out and grabs you, doesn't it?' he said.

Stephanie swallowed hard. Unwilling to make a fool of herself, she deliberately looked around the room, ignoring the play of light. 'It's absolutely impossible, Jordan,' she said. 'The floors creak, the kitchen is a wreck, it's so filthy that it will take a fire hose to clean it—'

He didn't seem to have heard her protest. 'For me,' he said thoughtfully, 'it was the way it stood here proudly, even though it had been deserted. When I first caught sight of it, I knew it was waiting for me.'

'Well, both of you may have a long time to wait,' Stephanie said practically. 'What's through that door?'

'The library.'

'Have you looked at it?'

Jordan looked thoughtful. 'No. I just know that's what it is.'

'You probably peeked in one of the windows.' Stephanie pushed the sliding door part way back into the wall recess, and looked in. The room was lined with shelves from floor to ceiling, and around the top of the room was a carved frieze of golden oak. A fireplace at one end looked big enough to roast an ox in.

'I don't believe it,' she said. 'All right. The library's wonderful, but I'll bet the bathrooms leave a lot to be desired.' She headed for the stairs, which curved upward through the tower.

There were five of them, and while they were antique, they were also charming. The one off the master bedroom was enormous. It opened on to a small dressing room, complete with a built-in glass-topped table concealed behind wardrobe doors. The adjoining sitting room looked out over the formal gardens. Stephanie was speechless as she stood there staring through the dusty window at what remained of a maze in the centre of the garden. It felt as if she was caught in a moment clipped from another age.

Jordan allowed himself a small smile. 'Ready to give up?' he said. 'You aren't going to talk me out of it, you know. This is the house I want.'

'Why? Sure, it could be elegant, with cream-coloured carpeting and classic art and good furniture. But why a big old house, Jordan? You don't need five bedrooms, plus servants' quarters, for heaven's sake!'

He looked a little uncomfortable, as if afraid that she would laugh. 'I've always wanted to come home to this kind of splendour, and I never had it. Now that I can afford it, only a house like Whiteoaks will fill the bill —because of the old-money atmosphere, I suppose. I could build something, but it wouldn't have the same appeal, because it would be brash and new. But an elegant lady like this one—'

'Right,' Stephanie said drily. 'Have you talked to Hallie McDonald?'

'Not yet. I'm sure you'll be able to work something out.'

'Why me?'

He raised an eyebrow. 'You do want a commission out of this, don't you?' He looked around the master bedroom appraisingly. 'I see the roof does leak, after all.'

But the patchy brown water stains on the wall didn't seem to bother him. At this point, Stephanie thought, if the floor had caved in under his feet he would merely have smiled and said that of course problems could be expected in older houses. She was fuming. If he had only felt this way about something that was actually for sale!

The old suspicion nagged at the back of her mind. Was it all just pretence, after all?

'I like having so many windows in the master bedroom,' he said. 'And the fireplace, of course. Think about it, Stephanie—lying on a rug in front of a blazing fire, making love on a cold night . . .'

The soft words wove a spell that hung like a jewelled web in the air, and for a moment Stephanie's throat was tight with nostalgia for those long-gone days when they had been together, when the world was new and fair, and all things were possible because they were young. Then she hardened her heart against the idea, and said, 'Do be a little cautious when you buy your rug, Jordan. A wool Oriental would be a bit scratchy, I'm afraid.' She retreated down the hall. 'Are you ready to go?'

'Don't you think we'd better check the attic for water stains? I want to know how much of a roof job I'll have to do.'

'Aren't we confident?' Stephanie said snappily.

Jordan smiled. 'Of course. I have hired what I am told is the best real estate person in town. Now we shall see if she really is.' He disappeared up the narrow stairs to the attic.

Stephanie had made up her mind to preserve her dignity and stay behind, but when long minutes passed and he didn't reappear, she went half-way up the steps. 'What happened? Did you get caught in a bear trap up here?'

'No, but I wouldn't be surprised if there's one around here somewhere. They seem to have everything else.'

That drew her, and she stopped at the head of the steps to let her eyes adjust to the dim light from the dormer windows.

'This is what I always thought an attic should look like,' Jordan said gleefully. He was half-way across the room, leaning on a steamer trunk.

Stephanie bumped into a dressmaker's dummy and automatically excused herself. 'You shouldn't be poking around through these things.'

'I want it written into the sales contract that all contents of the house go with it.'

'Be reasonable, Jordan. There are probably family treasures up here.' She picked her way across the floor and stopped beside what looked vaguely like a section of white iron fencing. It was an old bed frame, she saw —shoved up here after the family tired of it. It was without a doubt the biggest bed she had ever seen.

'Look,' he said. 'This is a family treasure?' He picked up a bonnet that must have dated from the turn of the century. The feathers had crumbled into dust, leaving only the spines sticking straight up from the felt brim.

'You know what I mean.' She scratched a fingernail idly across the bed frame and let out a shriek. 'I don't believe it. This thing is brass—and, from the age of it, probably solid brass. What idiot would have painted it white?'

'Shhh,' he cautioned. 'Maybe you'd better not look around any more. It will make your conscience uncomfortable.'

'My conscience is quite all right, thank you,' she snapped. 'Look at the posts on this thing. They're six inches thick and taller than I am.'

'Is that supposed to be good?' Jordan asked innocently. He dusted his hands off and started down the stairs.

'Do you want to make an offer on it?'

'The bed? That would depend on who else was on the bed at the time, actually.'

Stephanie fought down the blush that threatened to overwhelm her. 'I meant the house,' she said, careful to enunciate clearly. 'If you're going to make a fool of yourself about this house, we might as well have something definite to talk to the owners about.'

'Sure. Find out what it's valued at, and then offer them—oh, let's start with twice that.'

'Twice the—Don't you even know how much that would be, Jordan?'

'Not precisely. Should I?'

'I'll let you know,' Stephanie said tartly. 'I'd hate to make a fool of myself with an offer that you couldn't meet.'

He just smiled. At the door, as she was checking the lock, he looked up at the tower and said, 'Don't forget that I want to be living here by Christmas, Stephanie.'

'What if they still don't want to sell? And even if they do, it takes time for the negotiations and a closing and—'

'I don't see why it wouldn't be possible,' he said. 'There are all sorts of ways. Especially if you remember, my dear, that the sooner I have Whiteoaks, the sooner you won't have to bother with me any more. If you don't get it for me, you see, then I'm afraid I'll have to start looking all over again. And I just don't think I'll be very easy to please.'

CHAPTER NINE

STEPHANIE was putting the last few stitches in the hem of her new dress and trying, at the same time, to explain to Katie why she should not continue to treat Tony as an outcast.

'It's just not nice of you to refuse to talk to him, Katie,' she pointed out, and rethreaded her needle to sew the buttons on the cuffs.

Katie, who was undressing a doll in the middle of the floor, shrugged her shoulders as if to say, And who cares? It was a new doll and it had a large enough wardrobe to outfit the average baby; Jordan had brought her home with it after his last visit.

Stephanie exchanged glances with Julie. The baby-sitter was having trouble keeping a straight face. Then she asked, patiently, 'Why won't you talk to Tony, Katie?'

'He ran over my trike.'

'But it was an accident. And you did leave the tricycle in the driveway. If Tony hadn't come along just then, I'll bet your daddy wouldn't have seen it either, and he might have driven over it instead.'

Katie looked up then, eyes wide with astonishment. Then she shook her head firmly. 'Daddy would have looked for it.'

'Well, perhaps you're right.' If I was driving the kind of car Jordan does, she thought, I'd keep a pretty careful eye out for obstacles, too. 'At any rate, Tony did bring you another tricycle, Katie.' It was a nice one, too, but it had sat untouched in the garage since Tony had put it there. Katie had refused to ride it.

The child's lower lip protruded. 'I don't want it,' she announced. 'Trikes are for babies.'

'Then I suppose we might as well take it back to the store,' Stephanie said calmly, 'so that some other little girl who wants a tricycle can have one.'

That slowed Katie down for a moment, but before Stephanie had a chance to press her advantage, the telephone rang. Damn, she thought. Tony was picking her up in fifteen minutes, she was still sitting here in her slip trying to finish a dress so she didn't have to appear once more in one of her old ones, and now someone wanted to chat!

It was her mother. 'Sorry to rush you, Mom,' Stephanie said, 'but the Bruces are having a house-warming party tonight for the new house I sold them, and—'

'This will just take a minute, Stephanie. I was planning my menu for Thanksgiving dinner, and I wanted to make sure you and Katie hadn't made other plans. You will be spending the day with us, won't you?'

'We always do, Mom.'

'And what about Tony? Would he like to join us this year?'

Stephanie's hand tightened on the receiver. Her mother's voice had been calm, matter-of-fact. It was the first time in the months of Stephanie's engagement that Anne had included Tony in a family event. Was she finally going to accept him—perhaps even to support Stephanie's decision to marry him?

'I'll ask him tonight, but I'm sure he'd like that.' She cleared her throat and added, huskily, 'Thanks, Mom. It's important to me that you approve my choice.'

'I don't think I've gone quite that far, Stephanie.' Anne's tone was dry. 'I still don't like the man. But I'm willing to get to know him better, to keep peace in the family.'

'I'll let you know tomorrow if he's coming, Mom.' She

put the phone down with a vague feeling of uneasiness. They hadn't mentioned Tony's name, between them, since the day that Anne had told her why she didn't like him. It had been a subject neither had wanted to raise, but it had lain between them for weeks like a brick wall. Now, suddenly, Anne was inviting him to dinner. Stephanie wondered what her father thought about it. Or perhaps he didn't care. Holiday celebrations didn't seem to be as important to him, somehow, as they were to her mother.

'Oh, come off it and go finish your dress,' Stephanie lectured herself. 'And stop trying to figure it out. Mom just had a sudden attack of conscience, that's all, and realised that if she doesn't accept Tony she's likely to lose me. That's all it is. And I'm glad that she's finally coming around.'

She was knotting the last thread when the doorbell rang. 'Katie, answer the door, please, and be polite to Tony or I'll—' There was no threat dire enough, and no time to express it, either, for the bell pealed again demandingly.

'I'll keep her in line,' Julie promised, and Stephanie seized her dress and fled for the bedroom.

She liked to sew her own clothes, when she had time. She liked to know, when she walked into a room, that no other woman there would be wearing the same dress. But when she was under pressure, as she had been this time, everything seemed to go wrong. Needles broke, seams puckered, hems would not hang straight—

It was worth it, though, she decided as she looked over the dress in her mirror. The soft fabric draped beautifully at her slim throat and whispered as she turned to and fro to study herself from every angle. The pale apricot shade reflected colour into her face and seemed to make her auburn hair glow.

Tony was waiting impatiently. 'Couldn't you at least

be ready on time?' he growled when she came into the room.

Stephanie looked from him to Katie, who was sitting primly in a chair, her hands folded, and knew that most of his irritation was because of the child. Despite her promise, Julie had apparently not been able to keep Katie on her best behaviour. There was no sense in arguing with Tony about it, so she got her coat, gave Julie her instructions, and kissed Katie goodbye without a word to him.

'Have you talked to Hallie McDonald yet?' he asked as they got into the car.

'No, and I've spent the best part of two days trying to catch her.' She sighed. 'I'm about to give the whole thing up, Tony. There's no use in wasting all my time for a sale that will never come about.'

The silence in the car seemed to crackle. Then Tony said, 'You might remember that it isn't just a matter of a house for Kendall. There are thirty sales at stake here.'

Stephanie bit her lip, and then the words seemed to burst out. 'And I'm going to be the next Archbishop of Canterbury, too. Tony, when are you going to see what Jordan is doing—'

He cut firmly across her protest. 'If you lose this commission, Stephanie—or give up on it, which is even worse—you might just as well get out of the real estate business altogether. Once the word gets around that you quit when it gets tough, you'll never sell another house.'

There was no arguing with that. Tony might not have experience in the way Jordan Kendall's mind worked, but he certainly knew real estate. For the first time, Stephanie began to realise how very easy it would be for Jordan to ruin her professional reputation, with no more than a murmur or a raised eyebrow or a meaningful refusal to comment.

The devil, she thought. He set out to ruin me, and he

has closed off every avenue of escape. No matter what I do right now, he has me in his power. And then, the most dreadful thing of all occurred to her. Fear clutched her heart. When I have no income and no job left, she thought, then he might try to take Katie, too.

She tried to tell herself that it was all in her imagination. He couldn't take Katie, anyway, she thought. He would have to prove her an unfit mother.

Besides, she told herself roundly, he didn't have enough power to ruin her, to take her livelihood away. No one who had just arrived in town could have already developed so much influence. After all, her family had lived there for years, and her parents were prominent in the community. I have friends, too, Stephanie told herself firmly.

But it didn't take long for disillusionment to set in. The Bruces' housewarming was one of the events of the season, and the guest list read like the social register would have, had there been one in that little town. Among the guests were two people who were the centre of attention—Jordan Kendall and the woman in black who was next to him.

Stephanie's hands were suddenly clammy on the cocktail glass she clutched. The woman was gorgeous, her black hair upswept and an outrageous hat perched atop it. No other woman in the room would have dared to show herself in that hat, but on her it looked strangely appropriate. And she looked very comfortable on Jordan's arm, as well . . .

Next to that sleek and stylish designer gown, Stephanie felt very dowdy and cheap in her home-made dress. No other woman in the room was as well dressed, and most of them were, like Stephanie, eyeing the newcomer as if wondering how she managed to look so casually elegant.

Stephanie tugged at Tony's sleeve. 'Who is she?' she breathed.

It was impossible that Jordan had heard her. She was twenty feet from him, and between them were a dozen chattering guests. But as she asked her question, he looked up suddenly, laughing at something the woman had said, and his eyes met Stephanie's with sudden intensity. For an instant, it was as if the room had gone silent, and the question in his gaze was as clear as if he had shouted it. What's the matter, Stephanie, he was asking. Are you jealous?

And Stephanie knew, with a sudden clarity that rocked her to her toes, that the answer was yes. After all these years, she thought bemusedly, and when you least expect it, the wicked green monster strikes. She found herself thinking of all the things she would like to tell the woman, so she would no longer look up at Jordan with that warm gleam in her eyes. Stephanie would have liked to destroy that look, to destroy the woman, to destroy Jordan if that was what it took—

'She's your best hope for selling Whiteoaks,' Tony said.

Stephanie dragged her eyes away from the couple by the fire, and said, 'What did you say?'

'Don't you recognise her?' Tony asked. 'That is Tasha McDonald.'

For an instant, Stephanie was certain that she hadn't heard him correctly. That gorgeous creature—Jake and Hallie McDonald's daughter? 'That's impossible,' she said flatly. 'Tasha was a little brown mouse—'

'Was,' Tony agreed, and looked around for another drink. 'But she isn't any more. And it looks to me as if she might end up as Mrs Jordan Kendall.' There was a savage satisfaction in his voice.

'And if she wants Whiteoaks . . .' Stephanie murmured. Why should she be surprised? There are all kinds of ways, Jordan had said. It shouldn't come as a shock to her if Tasha was one of them. If anyone should know what Jordan was capable of, it should be Stephanie herself. And yet, it was a blow.

The babble around her was making her head ache. Stephanie wished fretfully for a moment that she hadn't come, and then told herself roundly that it was a good thing she had. In the meantime, of course, she reminded herself that she was being watched just as carefully as Jordan and Tasha were. She was being observed for any sign of uneasiness, or irritation that her ex-husband was here with his new girlfriend.

Stephanie put on a cheery smile, and turned to the woman next to her. 'They're an attractive couple, aren't they?' she said, with a flip of her hand.

And then she realised that the woman beside her was Hallie McDonald.

'They certainly are,' Mrs McDonald said, with a secretive smile. Her gaze turned speculatively to Stephanie, then, as if she was reluctant to look away from her daughter. 'I understand that you have been trying to reach me,' she said, very softly.

'Yes, Mrs McDonald, I have. I have a prospective buyer for Whiteoaks.'

'I see.' The woman's eyes were cold and thoughtful.

'I have a firm offer to give you.'

After a long moment of silence, Hallie McDonald smiled. It was not a charming smile. 'And I have one for you, young lady. But let's find a more private place to discuss it, shall we?'

Mrs McDonald led the way across the huge living room, stopping here and there for a word and a smile to one of the guests. Once in the bedroom wing, she opened the first door she came to and unceremoniously ushered Stephanie inside.

'You want to know what it will take to convince me to sell Whiteoaks,' Mrs McDonald said firmly.

Stephanie nodded. 'I have a client who—'

'Well, I can't blame you for trying. You're certainly not the first real estate person who has attempted the job. It would make a nice commission, even at the reduced rate you are no doubt offering.'

'The offer is more than fair,' Stephanie said. 'In fact, it's quite high, considering the condition of the house and—'

The woman cut smoothly across Stephanie's words. 'And I want to know what it will take to convince you to leave Jordan Kendall alone.'

Stephanie's jaw dropped. 'I don't seek him out, Mrs McDonald,' she protested. 'He came to this town by his own choice. I certainly didn't pursue him.'

Hallie McDonald's smile was not a pretty sight. 'Spare me, Stephanie,' she said. 'He wouldn't be spending so many evenings at your house if he wasn't getting some encouragement. Now, what is your price for getting out of his life?'

'What do you mean by getting out of his life? Moving out of town? Running away?'

'Why not? You left him behind once before.'

'I think you've been misinformed, Mrs McDonald. I don't run away.' Stephanie swallowed hard. 'Besides, he is my little girl's father,' she pointed out. 'It's her that he comes to see. It's hardly a relationship that can be ignored—'

'But he's done quite well without her for several years. He can do so again. I understand your house is for sale, Stephanie. Well, I'll buy it, and give you quite a nice sum to help you start again, somewhere else—'

'No, Mrs McDonald. I do not take bribes.'

There was a long silence. Then Hallie McDonald said, 'Whiteoaks is not for sale, Stephanie. Not at any price.' She moved majestically to the door. On the threshold, she paused. 'I shall, of course, deny having had this conversation.'

'That's quite all right, Mrs McDonald,' Stephanie returned. 'I'm not wild myself about letting anyone find out that you thought I was so cheap.'

And then she made a stab in the dark. She had told Beth Anderson only that she wanted to show a client through Whiteoaks; she had not said who it was. She hadn't even told her parents. Only Tony knew, and that was the kind of knowledge that was never shared outside the office. And with all of Jordan's comments about it being her job, not his, to talk to Hallie—People might be guessing who it was who wanted to buy Whiteoaks, but no one knew for sure . . .

'Perhaps you'd like to know who the prospective buyer is, Mrs McDonald?' she asked sweetly.

'It makes no difference, Stephanie. I've told you that Whiteoaks is not—'

'It's Jordan Kendall. And the offer is twice the appraised value. Please think about it. It would let you make a marvellous contribution to the historical society.' She brushed past Mrs McDonald, who was standing as if frozen in the doorway, and went back to the party.

She tried to take part in the hilarity, to admire the decorating scheme that had brought the Bruces' new house to life, to be an ordinary guest at a housewarming party. But she felt like a piece of hand-blown crystal, so delicate that if anyone bumped against her she would shatter. She felt as if she had been attacked, there in that quiet room, as if her soul had been shredded and ripped and left to bleed.

Then indignation began to rise inside her. How dare Hallie McDonald make such an insulting suggestion? How dare she try to buy Stephanie off, to try to bribe her to leave the little town she had grown up in? How dare she try to purchase Jordan for her daughter . . .

Jordan. The crush of the crowd brought them close together, and Stephanie murmured, 'I need to talk to you.'

'I'll stop by after the party.'

She opened her mouth to protest. It was, after all, not urgent—but he was gone, taking Tasha out on to the makeshift dance floor in the middle of the family room leaving Stephanie alone.

The loneliness was like a cloud that insulated her from the rest of the guests. She fought against it, trying to laugh it away. How funny were the ways in which the human mind worked, she told herself. That sudden, crushing loneliness when he had moved away from her . . . It was silly to feel lonely because she wasn't the one who was dancing with Jordan, when she had been divorced from him for four years. The sudden, bitter jealousy when she had first seen Tasha McDonald beside him . . . When she herself was engaged to Tony, it was ridiculous to think that Jordan was being somehow disloyal to date another woman.

I'm concerned for Katie, she told herself. Jordan would eventually marry again, she thought, and probably he would have a family. Why else would he want the big house? It was, after all, the expected thing for a man in his position to do. His new wife, with a family of her own, would not want to be bothered with the child of his first marriage.

And then, Stephanie thought, Katie will be the left-over child, the one who doesn't fit in, the one who is different—

We'll have to make sure, Tony and I, that Katie doesn't come to rely too much on Jordan, she told herself firmly.

'Why so quiet?' Tony brought her another glass of champagne.

'Just thinking.'

'This is hardly the place to do it.'

And not the place to discuss Katie, either, she thought. Somehow, very soon, she had to make Tony understand how tragically important it was that he win that little girl's love. But this was neither the time nor the place.

'I've been turning something over in my mind,' Tony said, a little awkwardly. 'You've been so quiet, ever since we talked about the Anderson house and how I didn't think we could afford it—'

Stephanie absently sipped her champagne. She was scarcely listening. Across the room, Tasha McDonald was laughing up at Jordan. She's lovely, Stephanie thought. How she has changed from being that little brown mouse when we were at school . . .

'I've been figuring it out, and maybe we can,' Tony said.

She blinked up at him. 'Maybe we can do what?' she asked blankly.

'Buy the Anderson house.'

She should have felt a wave of triumph, a spark of gladness that they would have a nice home in a good location—a house she could be proud to raise Katie in. But there was nothing but a dull ache in her chest at the idea. Jordan had ruined that dream, too, she thought. Jordan's ghost would haunt me there.

'If we can get a good enough profit out of yours, we can swing the payments,' Tony went on. 'You were right.'

And the easiest way is to make a deal with Hallie McDonald, Stephanie thought. All I have to do is give up Jordan—

What a laugh, she told herself bleakly. As if I owned him! As if I ever possessed him at all. In all the time we were together we were never a couple, we were just two people who were sharing a pathway for a little while . . .

And why was Hallie making deals of that sort, anyway, she wondered. From all appearances, Tasha had Jordan in her pocket. Of course, appearances could be deceiving, Stephanie told herself. She had once thought that Jordan adored her, too, and she had been disillusioned.

So why hadn't she accepted Hallie's offer? At least listened to the whole thing? The money would be nice and, after all, it wasn't as if making that deal would actually hurt anyone. She didn't even know what Hallie had intended to offer.

Because it wouldn't have been honest, she told herself. Because I intend to stay here and marry Tony.

And because, deep down, I don't want to give Jordan up.

The words seemed to echo through her brain, and she shook her head wildly, trying to make the thought go away. How silly, she told herself. That's all over. You don't want him back—

'Stephanie? Are you all right?'

Tony's voice seemed to come from a great distance. She looked up at him with an effort, and felt as if she was looking at a stranger.

'Shall I talk to Beth Anderson about it tonight? She's here.'

'About what?' she asked faintly.

'About buying the house. What's the matter with you?'

She shook her head. 'No,' she said firmly. 'No, don't say anything to her.'

Tony frowned. He looked puzzled, as if someone had just changed the rules of the game. 'But you wanted that house,' he pointed out.

She tore her eyes away from Jordan and Tasha, and looked up at him. 'We want a lot of things, Tony,' she said softly, painfully. 'But sometimes we cannot have them. And sometimes when we get something, we find it wasn't what we wanted after all . . .'

It was for Katie. That was why she didn't want to break off all ties with Jordan, Stephanie told herself as she paced the floor that night. The house was quiet, and in the front bedroom Katie was a sleeping angel. But

Stephanie was agitated, too nervous to sleep.

He had said he would come by after the party. But midnight had come and gone, and there was no Jordan. He must still be with Tasha, she told herself, and tried to pretend that it didn't matter.

But it would matter to Katie. And Stephanie did not want Katie to be hurt. She chewed absently on a knuckle and said aloud, 'He's her father. It wouldn't be fair to cheat her out of knowing him—'

And then she heard what she had said. That was precisely what she had done four years ago, when she had refused to tell Jordan that he had a daughter. She had acted like a spoiled child, wanting her own way and, when she didn't get it, she had selfishly refused to share her toys—her baby.

But he had been selfish, too, she reminded herself. Jordan hadn't wanted to compromise, either, and the resulting war had made casualties of them both.

'A couple of children,' she said. 'We were selfish, spoiled children, not ready to be in love—'

Did she still love Jordan Kendall? Was that what had caused her so much pain tonight she saw him with Tasha?

'You don't have to love someone to be jealous,' she told herself firmly. Didn't they say that jealousy wasn't really love? It showed possessiveness, and immaturity, and insecurity. Real love meant that the other person was more important than oneself.

'If I had really loved him, I would have gone with him,' she said, painfully. 'It was so very important to him . . .'

But I did really love him, she thought. And perhaps I still do, in some remote way. I was his wife, I had his child. Those things don't go away. But memories don't make a good foundation for living.

A car door shut quietly in the driveway, but in the stillness of the night Stephanie heard it.

Jordan's breath was a cloud in the frosty air when she opened the door. 'You said you wanted to talk to me,' he said.

'It wasn't urgent. I certainly didn't mean that you had to come tonight.' And wait till Hallie McDonald hears about this, she thought. 'Perhaps we can talk tomorrow.'

'I've seen you in your nightgown before, you know. And without it, come to that. I'm not going to ravish you, Stephanie.' His voice was taut, as if he was saying it more to himself than to her.

She coloured, and then was furious with herself for showing any sign that she had even heard him. 'In that case, you might as well come in,' she said tartly. She shut the door firmly behind him and sat down primly in a straight-backed chair. 'I hope Hallie doesn't know where you are,' she said. 'She's unsympathetic enough without adding this to it.' Then she told him, briefly and without ornamentation, what Hallie McDonald had said at the party.

'So you see, Whiteoaks is not for sale,' she finished. 'That's the bottom line, Jordan.'

For a long moment, he seemed not to have heard her. 'You called me over here tonight to tell me that?'

'I certainly didn't do it for the charm of your company,' Stephanie snapped.

'You seem to have forgotten,' he said softly, 'that there are four owners. Why don't you start dealing with the other three?'

'Because without Hallie's share, you can't do a thing! You have to have all of it—'

'Well, let's start by getting some of it. Preferably in writing—options to buy will do well enough for now.'

'You're crazy, Jordan.' Unless, of course, she told herself, he expected Hallie's share to be a wedding present.

'Anything is for sale, at the right price,' he said, and

there was a sudden hard note in his voice that sent chills up her spine.

'Almost anything,' she corrected. 'Which is the other thing I want to talk to you about.'

'Oh?' They hadn't bothered to turn the lamps on, and only the dim glow of the street light oozing through the curtains interrupted the darkness of the room. His voice came quietly out of the darkness.

'Katie isn't for sale,' she said firmly. 'The big toys, the elaborate plans for your time together, the expensive clothes—you know very well I can't afford all that for her. Stop trying to buy her affection, Jordan.'

'I'll do what I want for Katie.'

'She's only a child. She doesn't understand the difference yet, and so when I can't do those things for her—'

'What are you asking me to do, Stephanie? Stop seeing her?'

I wish you would, she thought. It would make the inevitable so much easier . . . 'No,' she said. 'Just —don't see her quite so often, and don't give her so many things. Don't spoil her, and don't let her believe that some day she'll have you all of the time.'

The patter of bare feet was loud in the quiet house, and abruptly Katie appeared in the doorway. 'Mommy, there's monsters in my room,' she announced breathlessly. She started across to climb into Stephanie's lap. Then astonishment lit up her face. 'Daddy!' she squealed and threw herself into his arms.

'Hello, Peanut.' Jordan's eyes met Stephanie's with a gleam of triumph, over the dark brown head that was buried in his shoulder. 'Let's go get the monsters,' he said, ruffling Katie's hair, and took her back to her room.

Stephanie waited patiently. She heard rustling and giggles from Katie's room, and then silence. Finally, Jordan came back, carrying a paper bag. 'The monsters,' he said, with a wry smile. 'I put them in the bag so the garbage collectors can haul them away. It seemed to satisfy her.'

'For the moment, perhaps.' She refused to be distracted from the point. 'That's exactly what I mean,' she said quietly. 'Being a parent isn't an easy job, Jordan. It isn't all ice-cream sundaes and football games and bicycles. It's discipline and fevers and questions about where she came from and monsters in her room at night that can't be trapped in a paper bag—'

'Speaking of Katie's questions,' he said politely, 'just how do you explain Tony to her? It was quite obvious who she expected to see when she came out here.'

'Tony doesn't spend his nights here, if that's what you're implying,' she said tightly.

Jordan raised an eyebrow. 'I'm very glad to hear it. It tells me that you've maintained a shred of good sense, and that perhaps you'll wake up in time to avoid making the mistake of marrying him.'

'I don't see why you think that's any of your business, Jordan.'

'Don't you? Give me credit for being just as concerned about Katie as you are. Do what you like with your life, Stephanie. But when it comes to Katie—'

'Get out!' she said. 'I never want to see you again.'

'Oh, you'll see me. I'll pick her up as usual on Saturday.' The expression in his eyes dared her to object.

She shut the door behind him and leaned against it, unconcerned about the puff of frigid air that had swept in around her.

In a backward kind of way, she thought, she was glad that he had refused her request. Perhaps Katie was more important to him than she had expected. And if he kept coming to see her—

'Then I can see him, too.' The words were there, suddenly, hanging in the air, and for a moment Stephanie was unconscious that she had spoken them aloud.

Oh, my God, she thought, wearily. It wasn't just jealousy that was hurting me so badly at the party. It isn't for Katie's sake at all, but for me. I still love him, and I want him back . . .

CHAPTER TEN

AND it was far, far too late.

If she had known, on that first night at the club, how she really felt about him, there might have been a chance. If she had recognised, underneath the shock of seeing him again, the very real gladness that had flickered through her mind, they might have been able to salvage something from the wreckage. If she had only waited long enough to see the changes in him before she had let her temper flare, things might have been different.

But any chance they might have had for a second try was gone, ended in the bitter words Stephanie herself had flung at him. 'I never want to see you again,' she had said, and at that instant she had meant it. And thus any possibility of a reconciliation had died.

Oh, don't be ridiculous, she told herself angrily. All of these guilty thoughts assumed that she was the only one at fault, that Jordan would have been anxious to resume their marriage, that it was she who had sabotaged it. And that was plainly preposterous. He had been furious on that first night, in the country club dining room, as though she had somehow planned to plunge them into that public scene.

No, Jordan had not been interested in taking up their marriage again. And neither was she, she told herself robustly. Not really—not seriously. 'You can be attracted to a man, perhaps even love him in some aloof way, without wanting to live with him,' she decided. So what if she had discovered a lingering tenderness, deep in her heart, for the man who had been her husband, who was the father of her child? That was to be expected. It didn't mean that she could not bear to live without him. It didn't mean that the life she had planned for herself was suddenly to be thrown to the winds.

'You've done without him very well for more than four years,' she told herself sternly, 'and you can continue.'

What was it she had told Tony tonight? Something about people not always getting what they wanted, and sometimes when they got it, finding that it wasn't what they wanted at all. She had wanted Jordan so badly in the beginning, and then she had discovered that he was not all she had thought he should be. It should come as no surprise that she had nearly fallen into that same trap again.

And on that note, with the feeling that her head was going to come apart if she didn't stop thinking about it, she finally went to bed, and dreamed of wicked green monsters that chased her down the long halls of Whiteoaks, while Hallie McDonald's laugh echoed through the empty rooms.

She didn't see him again till the weekend, when he came to take Katie swimming at the country club pool. Stephanie was a little afraid when he came to the door, frightened that coming face to face with him again might dredge up the feelings she had buried in the last few days. How embarrassing it would be if he could see inside her heart!

But he was cool and polite, and she relaxed a little. Perhaps the whole thing had been in her imagination after all, those dreadful moments when she had thought she actually loved him. It had been silly of her to be so upset, she thought.

Katie appeared with her swimsuit and towel. She was anxious to try out the heated pool. She had been pestering Stephanie about it for days, and Stephanie was just a tiny bit jealous. She had expected that it would be she and Tony who would take Katie swimming there first. But of course Jordan belonged to the country club. He had joined right away; it was, after all, expected of a man in his position. Stephanie found herself wondering just how many other things would be expected of him, and whether he would comply.

Katie got her coat, but she was surprisingly reluctant to leave. 'Mommy, come with us,' she begged.

Before Stephanie had a chance to answer, Jordan frowned and said firmly, 'No, Katie. That's out of the question.' He had not even glanced at Stephanie.

It hit Stephanie like a rock in the stomach. Not that she wanted to go to the club, of course, but did he have to make it quite so plain that he wanted nothing to do with her?

She swallowed hard and then reminded herself that it didn't matter what Jordan thought of her. All she wanted was to get their business dealings completed, and then set her life in order again. 'I have those options you wanted,' she said. 'On Whiteoaks.'

He turned at the door. 'All three of them?'

'The two distant cousins agreed without hesitation, and of course Beth is anxious to get rid of her share. Her signed option is at the office, and the others will be coming in the mail any day. You can drop off the deposit money and pick them up whenever you like.' She hesitated, and then said curiously, 'What are you going to do with them, Jordan? Without Hallie's share, it will do you no good to have the options.'

His voice was cool, distant. 'I expect you'll eventually work something out with Hallie.'

It struck her hard. It wasn't easy to accept, that he was trying to get rid of her. 'Are you suggesting that I take her up on her offer?' Stephanie said finally. Her voice was husky, and it trembled just a little.

There was a long silence. 'It might have been a very interesting proposition,' he said.

She licked her dry lips, and struck back. 'I don't take bribes, Jordan. Especially for doing something that I'd do anyway. I hope you do get Whiteoaks, and soon, because I want to be rid of you.'

His jaw tightened. Then he bent to button Katie's coat. 'If that's what you really want, Stephanie, then you made one mistake.' He stroked Katie's dark hair slowly and said, 'Because we still have this one thing in common, my dear.'

The unspoken threat stayed in the air long after he was gone. It seemed to bounce off the walls and echo in her ears. 'Oh, stop it!' she told herself sternly. It was pointless to worry about it. In any case, she had asked for it. She had started the vicious slashing; he had merely finished it. If she had needed proof that nothing had really changed, she thought, that should be it.

Then she tied a scarf over her hair and put on her oldest faded jeans and started to clean the house. It was the only way she knew to work out frustration—to attack dust and dirt and the junk that seemed to accumulate and multiply in the drawers and dark corners of even the best-run kitchen. It all needed to be done soon, anyway, she told herself, so that the last-minute work would be easier when the house was sold.

For it would still be sold. She had changed her mind about the Anderson house, but there would be another house for her and Tony, one in which there would be no memories of Jordan. She only hoped that they would find it soon.

She was sitting on top of the refrigerator, wiping the dust off the highest cabinet shelves, when the doorbell rang. Tony, perhaps, she wondered as she climbed down from her perch. He knew, of course, that it was Katie's day with Jordan.

She caught a glimpse of dark hair and a brilliant red coat on the front steps, and she drew a horrified breath. If there was one person she didn't want to see today, with cobwebs and dust decorating her from head to foot, it was Tasha McDonald. But the only alternative was to pretend that no one was home.

The bell pealed again. Tasha apparently would not be easily convinced that she was an unwanted guest. Stephanie sighed and opened the door.

'May I come in?' Tasha asked politely. But she was in the living room before Stephanie could have framed a refusal. 'I thought I'd stop by and beg a cup of coffee, and catch up on everything that's happened. It's been years since I've seen you, Stephanie. I've never had time on my visits to look up old friends.'

So we've suddenly become old friends, Stephanie thought. And my aunt is a rhinoceros, too, she added inelegantly. 'Let's take the gloves off, Tasha,' she said. 'You're here to find out what I intend to do about Jordan, and perhaps to renew your mother's very generous offer. I'm not interested in talking about either subject, so why don't you just toddle downtown and buy a new dress, or something, so you won't have wasted the trip.'

Tasha smiled coldly. 'You needn't be crude, Stephanie.'

'This is my house, so I'll do what I please.'

'Goodness,' Tasha said mildly. 'If you treated Jordan that way—'

Stephanie looked at her for a long moment. 'You know, Tasha, it really amazes me.'

'What does?'

'The McDonalds have always insisted on the best of everything. And yet, you'd settle for a used husband.'

Tasha walked across the living room, the graceful, sinuous movements of a model looking quite out of place. 'We all make mistakes in our youth,' she pointed out. 'You did—and Jordan certainly did.' Her eyes, bright and assessing, slid over Stephanie's dusty clothes with contempt. 'Just don't compound your mistake by thinking that Jordan will ever come back to you.'

Stephanie let the silence lengthen. 'Perhaps you should ask yourself,' she said gently, 'why on earth I would want him back. Your mother seems to be under the same delusion. Tell her for me, please, that she has things backwards.'

Tasha raised a perfectly arched eyebrow. 'Backwards? I don't quite understand.'

'I don't expect that she would believe me. But she could ask him, if she'd like. Jordan will be done with me just as soon as he owns Whiteoaks.'

A gleam of excitement sparkled in Tasha's eyes. 'Jordan wants Whiteoaks?'

'Didn't she tell you? The longer she holds out, the longer he'll be spending time with me.'

'It's strictly business—the time he spends with you?' Tasha sounded doubtful. Then she took another long, assessing look at Stephanie. It seemed to reassure her. 'Yes, I believe you.'

'Thank you,' Stephanie said. She wanted to pick up the nearest blunt object and heave it at the girl.

'Though why he wants that decrepit old house, I don't understand,' Tasha murmured. Then she shrugged. 'Well, if he wants it, that's good enough for me.' She turned towards the door and said, with her model's smile, 'It's been so nice talking to you, Stephanie. I hope we'll be friends, if you decide to stay here.'

About the same time as the sun starts rising in the north, Stephanie thought. She went back to her kitchen cleaning with renewed vigour, seeing Tasha's face in every spot of dirt and taking great pleasure in destroying each one.

She had never really liked the girl. In childhood, she had disliked the shy timidity that made Tasha go along with her mother's plans, instead of being just one of the girls. Now, Tasha was exactly like Hallie—a social-climbing, mean, petty, vindictive little dictator. And she had decided that she wanted Jordan. Stephanie wondered if Jordan could see past that brittle, lovely surface to the shallowness underneath. 'If he can't,' she told herself, 'then he deserves to have to live with her.' She scrubbed even harder, and told herself that she didn't care. It was his life, and if he wanted to ruin it by marrying Tasha McDonald, that was certainly his privilege.

Tony stopped by a little later. Stephanie had emptied every shelf by then and she was up to her eyebrows in boxes and cans. 'Where's the coffee pot?' he asked.

'It's behind the wholewheat flour. Pour me some, too, would you?'

'Sure, if I can find a cup. You have dust on your nose.'

'It's probably not the only place.' She came down off her ladder and sat down with a sigh. 'I didn't realise how long I've been working without a break.'

'I suppose when we get the Anderson house we'll need a cleaning lady.'

'I'd never given it a thought, actually. But it would be a good idea, Tony.' Then she said, 'Wait a minute. Did you say, the Anderson house?'

'Sure. I talked to Beth yesterday, and made an offer—'

'But I told you I didn't want that house any more!'

Tony looked astonished. 'You must be joking! After all the fuss you made about that house, now you say you don't want it?'

'That's right. I don't want it.'

'Why not? What changed your mind?'

Because it's haunted . . . The words rang so clearly in her own ears that for a moment she was afraid she had spoken them. She went to the kitchen to refill her cup. With her back to him, she said, 'It just wasn't as nice as I thought it was.'

'Yeah. And now we're stuck because I've made an offer on it.'

'Correction,' she said as she came back to the living room. 'You're stuck, Tony. I told you quite plainly that night that I didn't want—'

'To be honest, I thought you'd just had a little too much champagne that night.'

She was furious. 'Tony, have you ever known me to drink too much? If you would just listen—'

'You weren't doing too well at listening yourself that night, you know. All you could see was Kendall with the McDonald hussy. Frankly, Stephanie, it was a little embarrassing for me—my fiancée with eyes only for her ex-husband, the bum who left her years ago—'

'He is not a bum!' For an instant they were squared off, and Stephanie's breath was coming hard. I can't believe I am doing this, she thought in some remote, detached corner of her mind. I am standing here defending Jordan . . .

Katie pushed the front door open. She was chattering at a slower rate than usual, and Stephanie glanced at Jordan for an explanation.

'She swam herself to exhaustion,' he said. 'I think a nap might be in order.'

'Don't want to take a nap.' Katie shook her head definitely, and then spoiled the effect by yawning.

'Nevertheless . . .' Jordan murmured, and guided her towards her bedroom.

'Certainly acts as if he feels at home, doesn't he?' Tony muttered.

She was darned if she'd admit to Tony right now how irritated she sometimes felt by Jordan making himself comfortable in her house without invitation. 'He is her father.'

'But he's not your husband. And if I'm going to have to play second fiddle to that con artist—'

'That's funny. You didn't think he was a con artist when he came to town, and started talking about the commissions on thirty houses.'

'That was before he started manipulating—'

'Don't let me spoil your argument,' Jordan said pleasantly from the doorway. 'But Katie wants her blanket.'

'It's in the drier,' Stephanie told him, and started to stand up.

'Don't bother, my dear,' he said. 'I'll get it.' He went off, whistling.

She saw the red, angry light come into Tony's eyes, and knew that Jordan had heard every word of that brief exchange. She maintained an icy silence until he had retrieved Katie's blanket, clean and fluffy and still warm from the drier in the basement, and had taken it into her room.

'Tony, you're seeing this all wrong,' she said, miserably. 'You just said yourself he's a manipulator. Don't you see? That's what he's doing—'

The telephone rang shrilly, and Stephanie jumped. That's all I need right now, she thought. Stuck between these two men, with one of them about to do murder and the other needling the situation, and now someone else wants something!

'Is this Stephanie Kendall?' asked the pleasant, well-bred voice on the other end of the line.

Stephanie froze. 'Yes, Mrs McDonald.'

'Well, it's so pleasant to talk to you, my dear. Now that I've had a chance to think over your offer, Stephanie—'

It didn't take long for Tasha to get home, Stephanie thought. She was a little stunned, because she hadn't dreamed that those few words to Tasha could make so much difference.

'I'm very interested in selling Whiteoaks to Mr Kendall,' Hallie McDonald said smoothly.

Stephanie swallowed hard. 'Is the price satisfactory?' she said. She hardly recognised her own voice.

'Oh, quite, my dear.'

'Then I'll have Mr Kendall sign the formal offer, and drop it off at your house tonight, Mrs McDonald, if that would be convenient.'

'Well, I don't know that there is any hurry—'

There is for me, Stephanie thought. Your name on that piece of paper doesn't actually mean much, but it will help to keep you from changing your mind. And I'm not about to let this one slip out of my fingers. It means too much to me—freedom from Jordan, most of all.

'Since the house is empty,' she continued smoothly, 'and Mr Kendall is quite anxious to move in, shall we set the closing date for next Friday? That's the day after the Thanksgiving holiday—' She was making frantic motions to Tony, who checked his calendar and nodded his understanding. The sooner the better, just in case someone got cold feet. She hoped that Jordan would agree to that, and suddenly realised that she had never asked him if he had made arrangements for his mortgage yet.

She looked up and realised that he was watching her. He was leaning against the door jamb with his arms folded. 'Can you have the cash by Friday?' she asked quietly, cupping her hand over the phone.

He nodded. There was no triumph in his eyes, not much of an expression of any kind, she thought.

Hallie was hesitant. 'There are three others to be considered, Stephanie. Perhaps—'

'I know,' Stephanie said in dulcet tones. How she would love to wave those options under Hallie's nose! But she didn't dare risk that sale. 'I'll talk to them right away, and if there is any problem, we can push the closing date back, of course.'

'Then—' Hallie's voice wavered, 'I suppose we might as well go ahead.'

Having the options was a stroke of brilliance, Stephanie thought. If they had to start negotiations now with the other three owners, by the time they had reached agreement, Hallie would almost certainly have changed her mind.

She put the phone down and said, 'Jordan, you just bought a house. You're a genius! Having those options already signed for the other three heirs—'

'You must have done something to change her mind,' he observed quietly.

'Oh. Yes, I did, sort of. I need to talk to you about that.'

For a moment it was as if they were the only two people in the world. It's over, she thought. As soon as Hallie signs those papers, it's over, and I won't see him again. Except for Katie, it will be as if we never were together, as if we never loved . . .

Tony cleared his throat. 'Well, I'll run along so you two can settle the details.' He shot a look at Jordan, and then put a possessive arm round Stephanie's shoulders. 'Goodbye, darling,' he said, and kissed her, long and passionately.

Stephanie was passive in his embrace, and finally he let her go. 'I'll see you later,' he said, and was gone without a word to Jordan.

What seemed like an hour passed, with the two of them just standing there, staring at each other. Then Jordan asked quietly, 'What did you do, Stephanie? Did you agree to Hallie's terms?'

Had he wanted her to do that? She laughed a little, nervously, and said, 'Not really, I just told Tasha what you'd said—that once you had Whiteoaks there would be no need for us to see each other again. She must have run straight home to tell her mother.'

There was a long silence. Then he said, very softly. 'Thank you for Whiteoaks, Stephanie.'

The tenderness in his voice was like a magnet, and she took a hesitant step towards him. 'It's my job—'

'Having that house is like having a dream come true for me. Part of my dreams, at least.'

And the other part, she wondered—what was it? Tasha? But at this moment, it didn't seem to matter. 'My business is selling dreams,' she whispered.

His mouth was tender, caressing. His lips travelled gently over her cheek, her eyelids, her temple, and then she sighed and relaxed in his arms as he took her mouth. Where Tony's kiss had demanded, Jordan's asked, almost pleaded. And Stephanie opened like a flower under that gentle caress.

For a long moment, it was as if some other woman was standing there, paralysed in his arms, unable to think of anything except this moment, wanting it to last forever.

Please, she was thinking. Pick me up, take me into the bedroom, and remind me what it was like to be your wife.

The fire was building in every cell of her body, screaming for his possession, for the ultimate physical closeness that was the only way to soothe the lonely ache inside her.

It was the only way they had ever found to express tenderness or caring. What, she wondered vaguely, made her think that this time would be any different? And then she remembered Tony, and the engagement ring she wore, and she realised how very close she had come to betraying the trust he had put in her. She tore herself from Jordan's arms. 'No,' she said, harshly, as much to herself as to him. 'Tony . . .'

Jordan's breathing was fast and shallow, but there was no other sign that he was feeling anything at all. He stood there and looked at her for a long time, and then said, very quietly, 'You're really going to do it, aren't you? You're going to marry him.'

'Why shouldn't I?' she said, her voice low and harsh. 'I'm not your wife any more. You don't own me.'

'I never did, Stephanie. But I probably know more about you than any other man alive. And I know that you can never be happy with Tony.'

'Why shouldn't I marry him? I care about him, and we have things in common. He's done so much for me—'

'Spoken like a woman truly in love,' he said. His voice was heavy with irony. 'Listen to what you're saying. At least be honest with yourself, Stephanie. You have doubts about whether you can be happy with Tony. When I kiss you—'

'The only thing we had in common we found in a bedroom, Jordan. Tony and I have our work, our interests—'

'Working together is no basis for marriage.'

She struck back. 'Neither is sleeping together—when that's all there is between two people!'

Jordan's jaw tightened. 'I never said it was,' he said coolly. 'But you've gone from one extreme to the other, Stephanie. You aren't attracted to Tony. His touch leaves you cold. I saw how you acted when he kissed you.'

'Oh, without a doubt, you're better at that,' she said sarcastically. 'But don't forget, Jordan, that sex isn't the only important thing.'

'But it can't be ignored, either,' he pointed out. 'And it is important to you. No woman who can respond as you do can be happy sleeping with a cold fish like Tony Malone.'

Did he really care? she wondered. Would it bother him if she was unhappy in her new marriage? Was there some spark left between them?

'For God's sake, Stephanie, don't do it,' he said, and his voice was low and pleading. 'Doesn't Katie's dislike of him mean anything to you? She instinctively dislikes the man.'

'She is jealous of him. That's all.'

'That is not all! She is afraid of him, she hates him—'

'And you've encouraged her!'

'I have not. It was a full-grown battle before I ever came into it.' He took a deep breath, and said, 'Look,

Stephanie, I don't give a damn what you do with your life. You're an adult, and you can mess it up however you please. But Katie is only a child—'

And Katie was the only thing that mattered to him. It answered her question, that was sure. Stephanie's traitorous body remembered those insane moments in his arms, when she would have agreed to anything he asked, and she shivered. He hadn't pressed her to make love with him, because he didn't want her in that way. He had kissed her only in the hope of making her think that she didn't love Tony enough to marry him.

He was a good actor, she thought bitterly. Broadway had lost a star when Jordan had decided to play with robots. If he had pressed on just a little further, if he had not stopped short at taking her to bed—

She didn't even want to think about that. But he had considered it, and he had known that if he made love to her today he might have trouble getting rid of her again. So he had only kissed her.

Only a kiss, she thought. It had been almost enough to sabotage her hopes for any kind of a normal future. She had been close to throwing away everything she had worked for in the last few years. And for what? For a man who had already walked out on her once.

She would have been furious, but there was no room left. Her heart was filled with bitterness instead.

She swallowed hard, and said, her voice absolutely level, 'I'll see you at the closing on Friday, at the office. And that will be the end of it. Goodbye, Jordan.'

It felt as if she was saying farewell to half of her life.

CHAPTER ELEVEN

NOVEMBER was drawing to a close. The brilliant leaves were gone, and the few that still managed to cling to the branches were dry and ugly brown. They rattled in the wind, the blank cold wind of winter that was just beginning.

It was the morning of Thanksgiving Day, the holiday when the entire nation seemed to skid to a halt to give thanks for the bounty of another harvest, another year. Katie was in the bath, singing an off-key song about the pilgrims that she had learned in preschool.

Stephanie put her head round the door. 'Come on, little fish. Out of the water so you'll be ready when Tony comes to pick us up.'

Katie stuck her lower lip out. 'Does he have to come?'

'Grandma invited him to Thanksgiving dinner this year. Do you want to wear your new blue dress?'

Katie forgot Tony. 'The one Daddy got me?' She climbed out of the tub. Stephanie dried her off and was rewarded with a hug. 'I love you, Mommy.'

Stephanie's throat tightened. Funny, she thought, how such a little thing could change the mood of a whole morning. Before that hug, the only thing she had been thankful for was that tomorrow the sale of Whiteoaks would be final, and so far it looked as if no one on either side would back out. Now— She held Katie close, breathing in the scent of baby shampoo. Yes, she had plenty of blessings to count, the main one being this child in her arms.

Katie wriggled. 'Mommy,' she giggled, 'you tickle my neck!'

What was best for Katie? It was a question that

Stephanie had struggled with in the past few days, since the last time she had seen Jordan. 'Katie is only a child,' he had said. But did that mean that she must consider only Katie's welfare? What about Stephanie's own needs? And when the two things collided, then what?

Katie looked quite grown up in her powder blue velvet dress. Jordan never stopped with half measures, Stephanie had to admit. Many fathers would have bought only the dress. But Katie had come home with frilly petticoat, tights, black patent shoes, and a matching blue velvet bow for her hair, too.

I ought to resent it, Stephanie thought. For years, I've wanted to dress her like this, and I never could afford to. But she couldn't bring herself to be angry when she saw Katie's dark blue eyes sparkling as she inspected herself in the mirror.

'I'm pretty!' Katie said, with a note of discovery in her voice.

'You certainly are, darling. Grandma will be impressed.'

She left Katie turning back and forth to admire herself in the mirror, and went to finish dressing. Stephanie had a new outfit, too, a pale pink suit with a feminine, frilly blouse. The colour should have clashed with her hair, but instead it brought out the coppery sheen. It had cost the earth, at least by Stephanie's standards, and she had bought it on the strength of tomorrow's sale. 'If you back out, Hallie McDonald,' she muttered to herself, 'and cheat me out of my commission, we'll have another score to settle!'

It was so much fun to have a new outfit, one that she hadn't made, one that would stand up even if compared to Tasha McDonald's wardrobe . . .

Stephanie had just given the final brush to her hair when the doorbell rang. She sighed in relief. At least they wouldn't keep Tony waiting, as they had so often.

Katie was doing a pirouette for Tony in the middle of

the living room. 'Don't you think I'm pretty in my new dress?' she demanded.

Well, at least she's talking to him now, Stephanie thought. 'Katie, we don't ask for compliments,' she reminded her.

Katie thought that one over. 'But I am pretty,' she pointed out logically.

'And if someone tells you that, then you smile and say thank you. But you may not—'

'I see the clothing stores downtown can stay in business for another month,' Tony said. His eyes were on the pink suit.

Stephanie bit her tongue.

'And as for the blue velvet dress, Stephanie—what a ridiculous thing to buy. She'll outgrow it before she's worn it a half dozen times.'

'Probably,' Stephanie agreed stiffly. She got her last-year's winter coat from the cupboard, and handed Katie's white fur one down to her.

Tony's eyes started to bulge at the sight of the fur coat. 'I don't believe it,' he said. 'Give you a bit of money and you go crazy. I can't bear to think of what you'll do after that commission is paid tomorrow.'

'Then don't think about it,' Stephanie recommended. 'It is my money, after all.'

'But to waste it on things like that—'

Stephanie had listened to enough. 'When you are paying for Katie's clothes,' she said, 'then you will have a right to specify what she wears. In the meantime, it isn't any of your business.'

Tony opened and closed his mouth a few times, like a goldfish.

Stephanie put her coat on. 'Are we ready to go?' she asked. Her voice was polite, but the joy had gone out of the new clothes.

For the first time, Stephanie realised how deeply he resented Katie. Was it because Katie was Jordan's daughter, and not his, she wondered dispassionately. She had never expected him to adore Katie; few step-fathers did. But what about their own children? Would Tony resent any child who absorbed her time, her attention, her resources?

But of course, Katie hadn't made it easier. Why couldn't she be as sweetly charming to Tony as she was whenever Jordan was around? The little demon seemed to know exactly how to stab Tony in his most vulnerable spots, while with Jordan—

That's not quite true, Stephanie told herself. She's still a terror sometimes when Jordan is here. But she doesn't get attention for bad behaviour, so she cuts it out . . .

'Why in the bloody hell is that car in your parents' drive?'

'Please, Tony,' Stephanie said automatically, still absorbed in her thoughts. Then, as she saw the weak sunlight gleaming off the surface of a silver Lincoln, she sat up straight.

'Daddy's here!' Katie said gleefully from the back seat.

'He must have just stopped to talk to Dad about something,' she said uncertainly.

'He can't use the telephone?' Tony snapped. 'Why didn't you tell me he'd be here?'

'I didn't know,' Stephanie protested.

'Well, what is this? Some kind of family showdown?'

Katie was struggling with the catch of her seatbelt. 'Dammit,' she said, very clearly, when it wouldn't release.

Tony twisted around in his seat. 'What was that, young lady?' he demanded.

'Really, Tony.' Stephanie unfastened the belt and set Katie out on the pavement. The child ran for the front door. 'You've said much worse, and in front of her.'

'She is four years old!'

'Yes, and she knows now that all she has to do to get your attention is swear. Come on, Tony. It isn't the end of the world. Probably he just stopped in for eggnog or something. It's a family tradition.'

'Yeah. Just one big happy family.'

The aroma of roasting turkey was already permeating the house. Karl had seen the car, and he was waiting at the door for them. 'Happy Thanksgiving!' he said, and put a kiss on Stephanie's cheek.

Behind him, Jordan was rising to greet them, with Katie already in his arms.

He always had beautiful manners, Stephanie thought absently. I wonder where he ever learned them, considering the haphazard way he grew up . . .

Karl was busily taking coats and urging them towards the eggnog pitcher. He apparently didn't see the sparks that flew between the two younger men, but Stephanie did. For an instant, it felt as if the temperature in the room had dropped twenty degrees.

Katie broke the silence. 'Mommy says I'm not supposed to ask you if I'm pretty,' she confided to Jordan. 'So you have to tell me first!'

He laughed. 'You're not just pretty, Peanut,' he said. 'You are absolutely beautiful today!' But his eyes, as he spoke, were on Stephanie, skimming over the new suit, pausing at the halo of copper hair, and then resting on her face. The warmth in his eyes made her jittery, as if she was suddenly standing there naked in the middle of her parents' living room.

He's only doing it to make you feel uncomfortable, she told herself sternly. He's doing it on purpose.

'I'll see if Mom needs any help,' she said quietly.

She had to brush past Jordan to reach the hallway. He moved aside just enough to let her pass, and murmured, 'Running away, Stephanie?'

She tried to ignore him. Perhaps she was running

away. She felt as if she were deserting Tony, that was sure. But right now, Tony would have to fight his own battles.

Anne was bending over the oven, basting the turkey with butter. She straightened up as Stephanie came in and, though her voice was cheery, Stephanie could see the tension in the lines of her mother's face.

Stephanie didn't bother with greetings. 'What is Jordan doing here?' she demanded.

Anne closed her eyes as if to gather her strength. 'You know how unconcerned your father is about holidays, Stephanie—how he always tells me that whatever I plan is fine with him. So I invited Tony without consulting him, and he—'

'He invited Jordan without consulting you.' Stephanie sagged against the refrigerator.

'That's it.'

'And we have to put up with a whole day of it?'

'Well—' Anne tried to think of something positive. 'The turkey is almost done, and there's a football game on right after—'

'Tony hates football.'

'Oh, dear. I was afraid of something like that.' She sighed.

Karl put his head in the door. 'Is there another pitcher of eggnog, honey?'

Stephanie reached into the refrigerator. 'Dad, why did you invite Jordan?'

He looked puzzled. 'I hated to see him have to be alone on the holiday, Steph. Half the fun is having the family gathered around, and after all, with Katie here, you know—Now really, how enjoyable would holidays be for you if you didn't have Katie?'

'Dad, he's my ex-husband,' Stephanie pointed out. 'It's simply not done!'

'But that's just it, Steph,' he said, delighted that she understood. 'It's all over between you two, so why not be friends, for Katie's sake? For mine, come to that. He is my boss, you know.'

'That wasn't my choice,' Stephanie said tightly. Her father obviously didn't understand, and if she succeeded in explaining it to him, it would ruin his day, too. One person in this house might as well have a good time, she thought drearily.

'Want a glass of eggnog?' he asked brightly.

'Sure.' And put a couple of shots of rum in it, to help me through the day, she thought. But she didn't say it.

In the dining room, Katie scrambled for the chair next to Jordan's, not noticing that nobody else was contesting her for it. 'I'm hungry, Gramma,' she announced.

'Be careful not to spill that glass of grape juice,' Tony warned her, with heavy emphasis. 'If you do, you can't have any more.'

The twin looks of dislike from father and daughter would have been enough to send the average man whimpering out of the room, but Tony didn't notice. He was too busy spreading his napkin across his lap. 'This really looks good, Mrs Daniels,' he said cheerfully.

Jordan held Anne's chair with the casual grace that was part of him. 'Why, thank you, dear,' she said softly, and smiled up at him.

Karl was working the cork loose from a champagne bottle. 'Just a little something to celebrate with,' he said. 'After all, there's a lot to be thankful for this year.'

Not the least of which, Stephanie realised, was the change in him since he had started his new job. There was a spring in his step now, a sparkle in his eyes, a new zest as if each day was a fresh challenge. There might even be fewer wrinkles in his face, she thought.

Her eyes met Jordan's across the table, and she tried to telegraph him a silent thank you for his part in her father's rejuvenation. His gaze was level, steady, calm, and unsmiling.

The champagne cork popped, and Karl filled the

glasses around the table. He raised his glass and looked around in satisfaction. 'Get your grape juice, Katie,' he told her. 'Now, to all of us—to a happy year past, and another one ahead.'

Stephanie sipped her champagne. She could argue about the happiness of the past year, she thought, but she wouldn't.

'And to Stephanie, who has now got into the big time,' Tony said.

'Thank you,' she said. Unwillingly, as if he were a magnet, she looked across at Jordan. He raised his glass to drink the toast and his eyes met hers over the rim.

Then Karl said, really getting into the spirit of things, 'And let's drink to the wedding coming up. To Stephanie and Tony, best wishes for always.'

Stephanie heard her mother's sharp intake of breath. From the corner of her eye she could see Tony's beaming smile, in the moment before he raised his champagne glass. But she didn't really register the improper action; all she could see in that moment was Jordan.

He raised his glass, because it would have been obviously rude if he hadn't. But his eyes were hard as he looked across at her. It was as if he were saying, Nothing could make me drink to the health of your marriage, Stephanie.

Because of Katie, she thought. He had said that often enough. And he's right. For me to marry Tony would be the worst thing that could happen to Katie. I have to break it off. I have to get out of this engagement, as soon as possible.

But not for Katie. It would not be for Katie's sake at all, she realised. She stared into those compelling dark blue eyes across the table from her, and admitted to herself that she still loved him. She had always loved him, and she would always love him, and, for her, there would never be a man who could take the place of Jordan Kendall.

All the games she had played, all the excuses she had given herself, all the reasons she had so blithely recited for marrying Tony, had been worse than a joke. She had run from Jordan as far and as fast as she could, and had taken refuge in the person least like him. But it would work no longer, for she could not run from herself.

My God, she thought. How wonderful it would be, today, if it was just Jordan and Katie and me, and if, after dinner, we were taking our daughter home together . . .

Stephanie couldn't have swallowed right then if someone had held a gun to her head. All that I had, she thought, and I threw it away. Everything that I wanted, and because I didn't trust him and have faith in him, it's all gone.

For it was far too late now. Jordan had made that perfectly plain. Do as you like with your life, he had said, but don't mess up Katie's. He no longer cared about Stephanie. It was to be expected.

She was reeling from the shock of sudden knowledge. I should have known this weeks ago, she told herself. I should have realised, as soon as I saw him again, how important he was to me, and how much I still hurt because he left me behind.

Katie was getting the idea. 'Another one,' she said to her grandfather, tugging his sleeve.

He smiled down at her and tapped his crystal goblet against her tiny glass of grape juice. 'To Katie, the hope of the future,' he said gently. Katie beamed as they all drank.

To Katie, Stephanie thought. You've taught me patience, and love, and maturity. Now teach me forgiveness, and peace of mind, and hope for a future that looks very barren indeed.

'You know, Steph,' her father said, as he carved the steaming turkey, 'you really ought to get your broker's licence. Tony's right, you know. You are getting into the big time, and with all the new people coming to town, you might as well—'

Tony had stretched out a hand for a serving spoon that was out of Anne's reach. The idea of Stephanie as a broker seemed to give him a jolt. He darted a glance at Karl. His hand shook, and then, as he settled back into his chair, his sleeve caught on his wine glass, tipping it over with a crash.

There wasn't much champagne left, but what there was spread into a puddle on Anne's Irish linen table-cloth. Tony was red to the roots of his hair, stumbling over himself to apologise. Jordan was absolutely straight-faced, but there was a dangerous sparkle in his eyes.

Katie picked up her glass of milk, sipped it like a lady, and said politely, 'You can't have any more, Tony, because you spilled it.'

The look that Tony shot at her was confirmation for Stephanie. Even Karl looked a little shocked at the venom.

It wasn't that Tony was a villain, Stephanie tried to explain to herself. And he had been a great help in her career. But he was just so rigid about everything that Katie would suffocate. And so would I, Stephanie thought.

Then she realised with a shock that, if she had got her way, they'd have been married months ago, long before Jordan came to town. And then she would be sitting here at this table today, torn between husband and ex-husband—

I do owe Tony thanks for that, she thought. It's a backhanded sort of gratitude to feel, perhaps—but thank heaven I don't have another divorce to go through . . .

She stayed in the kitchen to help Anne with the dishes. After one look at Stephanie's set face, Anne stuck to neighbourhood gossip and unemotional conversation, chatting on even though Stephanie, absorbed in her own thoughts, responded only occasionally.

I have to break it to him right away, she thought. I can't stand to wait any longer.

But when she went into the living room, intending to bundle Katie up and take her home for a nap, she found the child sound asleep in Jordan's lap, her head snuggled into his shoulder while he watched the football game.

She bent over his chair. 'Do you suppose, if I lift her very carefully, that—'

'Why? She's quite comfortable.' His gaze summed her up. 'What's the matter, Stephanie? Are you anxious to get home?'

She could see what he was thinking. He assumed that she was planning to spend the rest of her holiday afternoon in bed. Well, let him think what he pleased, she told herself irritably. He was so very far from the truth that he would probably never understand.

'Go on if you like,' he said, and his eyes returned to the screen. 'I'll bring Katie home later. Will it be safe in a couple of hours?'

'Quite safe,' Stephanie said tightly.

Tony was agreeable. 'Football always did bore me to tears,' he said as they drove across town. 'I never did understand what civilised people saw in a brutal game like that.' He started to whistle a little tune.

Stephanie said, 'You sound very pleased with your-self.'

'Of course,' he said, surprised. 'I'm quite happy. I think I made a good impression on your parents today.'

'Absolutely,' Stephanie said drily, thinking of the wine stain on Anne's tablecloth.

'Your father seems to be really taking to me. Frankly, I didn't expect that. But they're really coming around. And even Kendall wasn't too bad to have around today.'

She didn't answer that, but she remembered the

angry, hurt look in Karl's eyes when he had seen how much Tony disliked Katie.

Oh, you made quite an impression, Tony, she thought.

She waited until they reached her house, but as soon as they were inside, she tossed her coat aside, squared her shoulders, and said, 'It isn't going to work, Tony.'

'What do you mean?'

She tugged the diamond ring off her finger. 'Our engagement. It's off.' She tried to soften the blunt statement. 'You're a wonderful guy, Tony, you really are, but we're not right for each other.'

'But, Stephanie—'

She hurried on. 'You've helped me a great deal, and I think I got confused between gratitude and love. No, that's not true, either. I think I do love you, in a way, but not the way—'

'The way you love Kendall?'

She said, her voice husky, 'That's all over, Tony.'

'Then why this?'

'Because I can't live the way you want me to, and I can't make the changes you're asking of me.' Her words were painful, sincere. It was hard to do, but better to have it done with now, to have a clean wound that could heal, not one that would fester. She had learned that much in her life—that bitterness brought no good to anyone.

'I've only wanted what's best for you, Stephanie.'

Harsh words trembled on her lips, but she swallowed them and said instead, 'I know that you had the best intentions always, Tony. But sometimes you treated me like a little girl. I'm a grown woman, and I have to make my own choices.'

He turned the diamond ring over and over in his hand. 'This is really the end of it, then?'

She nodded.

'What will you do, Stephanie?'

'I'd like to keep on selling houses, if—if you'll let me.'
For the first time, her knees were shaking. What if he
said no? What could she do to support herself and Katie?
Don't fret so, she told herself. With the commission on
Whiteoaks, you can look around a bit, find something
else to do—

'Sure. Why break up a good partnership?' His smile
was a little shaky, and for one split second she wondered
if she would regret this. Then she reminded herself of the
silent quarrels they had waged over the months. They
had never shouted at each other, but there had been a
hundred things she resented, things she had buried deep
inside herself rather than talk about . . .

'How I spend my money is up to me,' she reminded.

He nodded, slowly. 'But all I was trying to do—'

She was not going to argue with him, she was determined. 'Thank you for everything, Tony,' she said
firmly. 'I'll see you at the office tomorrow morning for
the closing.'

He sighed. 'Sure.' He picked up his hat, leaned over to
put one last gentle kiss on her lips.

The front door opened. 'Gramma sent a whole pan of
turkey for us,' Katie announced. She was holding it
carefully level.

Stephanie didn't hear. She could see only the cold
anger in Jordan's eyes, and she knew that he had seen
that last gentle caress and had jumped to the wrong
conclusion.

He didn't say a word. Before she had gathered her
senses, he was gone, the engine of the Lincoln roaring in
the drive and then racing off down the street. Two
minutes later, Tony had left as well, and Stephanie sank
down in the middle of the living room floor and cried till
there were no tears left.

They were all crammed into Tony's office for the closing. Whiteoaks had been so long without heat that they

would all have been frozen solid by the time the formalities were over. Stephanie knew that perfectly well, but she was still sad about it. It didn't seem appropriate, somehow, to be deciding the fate of that grand old house in a tiny office with half of the participants standing in the corners.

The closing went according to plan, but Stephanie didn't realise how frightened she had been until the last cashier's cheque was handed over and the last signature inked on the last dotted line. Then she released the breath she had been holding, and exchanged a smile with Tony. They had pulled off the deal that everyone had given up on long ago, and the cheque that he was holding represented several months' security for both of them.

Everyone was happy at a closing, Stephanie told herself. The seller was happy to be rid of a house, the buyer was delighted to own it, though perhaps still a little in shock at the size of the mortgage. She wondered for an instant if that was what was bothering Jordan today. She had expected that he would be elated at his new toy, but he didn't seem to have noticed that all the manoeuvring, all the planning, all the scheming, were over.

Tony looked happier than she had expected. She had braced herself for a pleading, whipped-puppy expression. She had even figured out what she would say if he asked her to reconsider her decision. But Tony was at ease. Was it possible, she wondered, that he was relieved to have the engagement at an end? It couldn't have been easy for him, either, she reflected.

Hallie McDonald was all smiles. 'Now you must invite us all to your first party at Whiteoaks,' she told Jordan archly. 'We'll all want to see its new glory.'

Beth Anderson was there, too. Technically, she didn't have to be present for the completion of the sale but, as she had murmured to Stephanie, 'I couldn't stand the suspense of sitting at home and wondering if it was really going to go through. So I came down, with full intentions of breaking both of Hallie's legs if she tried to back out.' She linked her arm in Tony's and drew him off to the side. 'I've been thinking about our decision to sell our house, and—'

Stephanie didn't hear the rest, but she hid a little smile. It looked as if Tony would get off the hook, too. That was some relief for her. She hadn't wanted to see Tony forced into buying a house he didn't want, and though he could have cancelled the deal, it would have been less than ethical.

She picked up her portfolio and started for the door. She had decided that she could afford to take the rest of the day off, and she didn't want to hang around any longer. Jordan had not said a word to her all through the formalities, and she was determined that she would not beg him to notice her. She had more dignity than that.

She was half-way to her car when he called her name.

She paused and gathered her poise. By the time she had turned round, he was half-way across the parking lot towards her, his hair ruffling in the breeze. He is so very handsome, she thought, and her heart ached for the days when he had belonged to her. Now—well, Hallie McDonald had made it coyly obvious in there that she hoped Tasha would be the hostess at Jordan's first party. And, Stephanie thought drearily, the woman might just be right.

What could Jordan want, she wondered. A formal end to the hostilities? A dinner or lunch together to celebrate? I'd choke on my food, she thought.

'Stephanie—' He broke off and ran a hand through his hair. 'You've more than fulfilled your part of the bargain. You'll be hearing from the rest of my people. They'll start to arrive right after Christmas, and they'll be anxious to get settled right away.'

'I'll brace myself for the rush,' she said drily.

There was another long silence, and then a sigh. 'I'll pick up Katie as usual tomorrow morning,' he said.

'I'll have her ready at ten.' Stephanie got into her car. 'Goodbye, Jordan,' she said. It was much more than a casual farewell to someone she would see again tomorrow. It was a farewell to a whole slice of her life, for tomorrow when he came to get Katie, it would be as ex-husband and nothing else.

Nothing else, ever, she told herself firmly. That's all gone, all past.

And she would be all right. Life didn't end simply because one avenue was closed off. She had Katie. She had her job. She had her house. That would be enough. It would have to be enough, she thought, with sudden fear, because there was nothing else.

She forced herself to smile at him, and wave a casual hand as she drove off. I'm not going to cry till I get home, she told herself. It was a noble effort, but it was in vain.

CHAPTER TWELVE

STEPHANIE was in the shower when the telephone rang. Darn it, she thought, at least on Saturdays a woman ought to be able to take a long, leisurely shower without being disturbed.

Then Katie pushed the bathroom door open. 'Daddy's on the phone,' she announced. 'He wants to talk to you.'

Jordan. For an instant, her heart sang, and then she deliberately put the damper on that joy. In the last two weeks, since the closing of the sale, she had seen him for only moments, when he had come to pick up Katie. He had been polite but quiet. There was no reason that today would be any different, she told herself.

'I don't suppose you thought to tell him that I'm dripping shampoo everywhere,' Stephanie said, but Katie had vanished. By the time Stephanie had rinsed her hair and wrapped a towel around it, found a bath sheet, and made her way to the living room, Katie had crawled back under the Christmas tree by the front window and was rattling packages.

Stephanie took her by the feet and dragged her out. 'No worming around under the tree,' she warned, and picked up the phone.

'Sorry about that,' Jordan said. 'She did say that you were in the shower, but by the time I told her not to bother you, she was gone. And she didn't come back to the phone.'

'You lost out to the attractions of the Christmas tree,' Stephanie told him.

'Well, I knew I couldn't be her hero forever. But I did hope it would last until she discovered boys. Being passed over for a tree is a bit of a shock. Anyway, I called to ask a favour.'

'I thought you'd get to the point eventually,' Stephanie said sweetly. She was beginning to feel cold in her damp bath sheet.

'I have workmen running in and out today, trying to get as much done as possible before the snow starts. At any rate, I can't leave. Is it possible that you could drop Katie off at Whiteoaks? I'll return her this evening.'

Stephanie glanced at the clock. 'Of course, but I'll be a while. I'm not dressed for the occasion at the moment.'

'I appreciate it, Steph.'

Her fingers clenched on the telephone. The nickname had come so easily to his lips, and it brought back so many memories . . .

'Nothing elegant in the way of clothes for Katie, I presume?'

Jordan laughed. 'She's apt to be covered in sawdust. They tore out the kitchen last week, and now they're starting to rebuild it.'

He sounds so happy, she thought as she put the phone down. Was it Whiteoaks that had brought that cadence to his voice? Or was it Tasha? She'd seen the woman around town several times. It seemed that Tasha had come home for good . . .

That line of thought will get you nowhere, Stephanie told herself firmly. She removed Katie from the tree once more, threatened to retrieve the playpen from the attic and put her in it if she didn't behave, and went to get dressed.

She rather hoped that she could get a glimpse inside Whiteoaks herself. She'd driven past it several times in the last two weeks, since the closing of the sale, and it was obvious that work was moving right along. The sagging wrought-iron gate had been straightened, the rubbish had been raked out of the yard, some of the trees and shrubs had been carefully pruned. But most of the outside work would have to wait till spring had returned.

Inside the house, however, it was apparently another story. The casement windows gleamed with light at all hours, a symbol of the rush that Jordan seemed to be in to have his castle complete. She had seen, parked in the back driveway, vans belonging to the plumber, the electrician, and the interior decorator. One day there had been a truck-load of carpet at the back door. She had wondered, with an almost personal concern, what colour it was, and then had abruptly told herself to be sensible. If Jordan wanted to carpet the place in leopard skin, it was none of her affair. And she had made it a point to stay out of the neighbourhood ever since, for her own peace of mind.

But today was different. She was, in a sense, an invited guest. In fact, Jordan might even ask her in to see the work. She did, after all, have a personal interest in the house.

There were workmen's trucks in the drive, but no sign of life as she stopped her little car. Katie was bouncing around as much as her safety belt allowed. 'Look, Mommy,' she said. 'There's the kitchen, and the dining room sticks out there, and—'

'Yes, darling, I know.'

Katie blinked. 'How?'

Deliver me from the questions of a four-year-old, Stephanie thought. 'I saw it once before your daddy bought it.'

'Oh.' Then Katie was off again. 'And there's my room, with the big windows—'

'Your room?' The panic-stricken question was out before Stephanie could stop herself.

Katie nodded. 'Daddy said I should have my own room in case I want to stay overnight.'

'Oh. I see.' It made perfect sense, she told herself. And it didn't necessarily mean that Jordan had any plans to take Katie away from her altogether. He was going to keep his promise, to recommend Stephanie to the new people who would be moving in. It was almost as if he was pushing business her way because he knew that she would refuse to take money directly from him.

'There's all the new stuff for the kitchen.' Katie pointed towards the open garage door.

'I see. I also see something that looks like a bicycle,' Stephanie said drily. The bike was tiny, with training wheels that looked nearly as large as the regular ones.

Katie chewed her bottom lip and looked up at Stephanie as though gauging how much trouble she was in. 'Daddy said if I didn't leave it in the driveway . . .' she offered hopefully.

'I should think you'd better not.' She reached across Katie to open the car door. 'You go ring the bell, and I'll wait here till you've gone in,' she said.

Katie planted a wet kiss on Stephanie's cheek. 'See ya later,' she promised. 'Don't go visit Santa Claus without me.'

'I wouldn't think of it,' Stephanie said.

So much for her hopes of seeing the work in progress, she thought, watching as Katie stretched on her tiptoes to reach the doorbell. She could have walked up to the door with the child, and invited herself in, but she was too proud for that. So she waited till Jordan answered the door. Then she returned his casual wave and backed the car into the street. She should know better than to be jealous of her own little daughter, she thought. But it hurt just a little to know that if she was to see Whiteoaks, she'd probably have to buy a ticket on the next charity tour.

The snow started in mid-afternoon, drifting down from the leaden sky. It caught Stephanie downtown, taking advantage of Katie's absence to finish the last of her shopping. The last few things were always the hardest, she thought. Her father, for instance, already had everything he wanted. She wandered through the men's clothing department, hoping that inspiration would strike.

Then she saw the sweater. It was the deep blue of a tropical bay—the colour of Jordan's eyes. She put out a tentative finger to stroke the soft yarn.

She hadn't even thought of buying him a gift. But he would of course buy things for Katie—

He's probably already spent a small fortune on her, Stephanie thought, so Katie should have something to give him.

She had the sweater wrapped and added it to her pile before she had a chance to talk herself out of it. What a silly thing to do, she told herself on the way home. Well, if she decided at the last minute not to go through with it, she could always return it.

But she put the brightly wrapped box under the tree as soon as she got home. It stood out, in its brilliant foil paper, nagging at her conscience. Be honest, Stephanie Kendall, it seemed to be saying. You didn't buy that sweater because of Katie. You bought it because you wanted to share a little bit of Christmas with him.

'Oh, shut up,' she told her conscience rudely, and went to fix herself a cup of tea and get into some more comfortable clothes.

'Speaking of Christmas,' she mused as she waited for the water to boil, 'perhaps after the first of the year you can afford a few Christmas presents to yourself.' She'd be staying in her little house now, of course. She'd go ahead with the dishwasher, and the new carpet in Katie's room. Maybe she'd even look into the cost of having the attic storeroom finished off into a sewing room. Heaven knew they could use the space and, with the commission she'd been paid on Whiteoaks, she could afford a luxury here and there.

It was getting late when the Lincoln's lights swept past the windows. Stephanie was sketching out the plans for the attic room, and she had her pencil between her teeth when she answered the door.

Katie swept in like a small tornado, chattering about the progress of the kitchen.

'Hush, Peanut,' her father told her. 'Mommy doesn't want to hear about the kitchen.' He looked at Stephanie and raised an eyebrow. 'I thought it was a rose that should be held between one's teeth, not a pencil.'

'Next best thing,' Stephanie said briefly. 'And as for the kitchen, how is it progressing?'

'Are you really interested?'

'Of course. I'm thinking of remodelling here.'

'You're going to keep your house?'

'Yes.' She kept her voice light, casual. 'Now that I'm not going to be married after all, Katie and I will stay here.' He nodded, and she realised that he had already known about her broken engagement. That shows you how much it really means to him, she thought. 'I'll learn from your mistakes so when I remodel my kitchen next spring it will be perfect.'

He scowled, mock seriously. 'Let me warn you, it isn't the most pleasant hobby I can think of. What would you like to know?'

Katie, unobserved, had wriggled under the tree. 'Mommy,' she called, 'what's this new package?'

'Katie, don't poke, please.'

'The shiny one. Who is it for?'

Stephanie looked thoughtfully at the foil-wrapped box. She hadn't put a tag on it. Perhaps she should just take it back—But what harm could it do to give him a simple gift? 'Are you going to have a Christmas tree, Jordan?'

'Probably,' he said. 'If all the workers are done in time.'

She reached for the package. 'Then put this under it—it's just a little something from Katie.'

Katie carefully backed out from under the tree and said innocently, 'What did I get him?'

Stephanie fought the blush that rose to her cheeks, and lost. She looked at the floor, and thought, You should have expected that one. Katie has never displayed tact, not one single time in her whole short life . . .

Jordan didn't smile. He shifted the package in his hands, and said, soberly, 'I'm sure Katie has wonderful taste. Thank you—both of you.'

Stephanie looked up at him, ready to explain, to tell him that she didn't expect any gifts in return, that she had only wanted Katie to have something to give—but there seemed to be no need. He read it in her eyes, and smiled, that heartbreakingly warm smile that she had seen so seldom in the last few weeks.

'Look,' he said, abruptly. 'I can talk all night about that kitchen, and draw diagrams, and sketch blueprints, and it still isn't going to be like seeing it. So why don't we drive over there so you can give it the full inspection?'

Her eyes glowed, and then she said, 'Oh, that isn't necessary, Jordan. It's a lot of trouble for you—'

'Would you like to see it, or wouldn't you?'

'I would, but—'

'Then go comb your hair.'

He sounded as if he was talking to Katie, for a moment. She went and combed her hair. Then, feeling incredibly silly, she traded her comfortable sweat-shirt for a more feminine blouse.

Jordan couldn't care less what she looked like, she scolded herself. But she cared, so she freshened her make-up, too.

Katie, of course, spotted it right away. 'You look pretty, Mommy,' she announced. She was sitting in the middle of the living-room floor, her rag doll and her blanket in her arms.

'Thank you, darling.'

'Very pretty,' Jordan said softly.

Stephanie blushed, and bent over Katie to fuss with

the buttons on her coat. 'Is it really necessary to take those things along? It will just be for a few minutes.'

'No big deal,' Jordan said.

'Well, if she leaves her blanket, I'll expect you to bring it right over so she can go to sleep.'

'She won't leave it,' he said cheerfully.

Now that it was too late to back out, Stephanie was getting cold feet. 'I could drive my car,' she offered. 'Then you wouldn't have to come all the way back over here.'

The snow was settling like icing on to his dark hair. He shrugged. 'There's no point in taking two cars out when the streets are icy.'

'We could go another time,' she said.

He quirked an eyebrow at her. 'Are you chickening out?'

She didn't answer. Her protests exhausted, she got into the Lincoln.

The streets were slick, but the heavy car negotiated them with ease. 'You're not exactly taking the most direct route, are you?' Stephanie asked.

'Depends on where we're going,' he said evasively, and turned the car into her parents' driveway. Before Stephanie had a chance to question him, he took a deep breath and said, 'It's late, and Katie has had a long day. So I called your mother and asked if she'd babysit for a little while.' He and Katie were on their way to the door before Stephanie could protest.

'You can't show me your kitchen with Katie there?' she asked when he got back into the car.

'It wouldn't be easy, let me tell you.' The snow was heavier now, large flakes reflecting the glare of the street lights. 'We also have some other things to talk about, and I'd rather not have her listening in.'

There was a note in his voice that brooked no argument. Things like where Katie would live? Stephanie wondered anxiously. But she didn't say anything until the car was safely in the garage. 'What sort of things?' she asked coolly.

'I changed my will, of course, as soon as I found out about Katie. As things stand, if something happens to me she'll be the richest four-year-old in town. But that's not the ideal situation . . .' His voice trailed off as he opened the back door. 'It takes a lot of imagination right now—but here's the famous kitchen.'

Stephanie had plenty of imagination. But all she had to do was half close her eyes to see the room as it would be. At the moment, of course, the floor was bare, and in the corners there were heaps of sawdust and discarded boards, pipes and electric wire. Part of the cabinets had been hung, and the mellowness of golden oak seemed to light up the room. The appliances were covered at the moment with a haze of dust, but they were obviously the best available. 'It looks a little like the kitchen in the Anderson house,' she said, finally.

'You might be right.' He sounded unconcerned.

'This will be nicer, of course.' She ran a hand across the ceramic tile behind the sink. 'It's lovely, Jordan.' How pleasant it would be to cook meals in this room, she thought, with sunshine pouring in the windows. I'd paint it yellow, she thought idly, and—Then she stopped herself. Tasha might paint it any colour at all.

'Would you like to see the rest of the house?'

She nodded, and followed him down the long hall. The warmth was the thing that tugged at her heart. What had been an old, cold, deserted house was now alive and humming and warm. It's got younger, she thought, now that it has a job to do again.

She stepped down into the drawing room, and her feet sank into the plush of cream-coloured carpet. She looked up with a question in her eyes.

'It sounded very pretty, when you mentioned it,' he said diffidently.

She nodded, and looked around, intrigued. There was

little furniture, no curtains. No personal items in the room. If this was what his interior decorator had done, Stephanie wasn't impressed.

'It isn't finished, of course,' he said. 'There's no point in doing much more until the dust is gone. They've tried to seal the kitchen off, but the dust creeps out anyway.'

'It is a little bare,' Stephanie said.

'Yes. I want to get some—feminine suggestions— before I go much further.' His voice was husky, as if he was having trouble phrasing the words. 'It's a little difficult to prepare a home for someone—'

She was glad that she wasn't looking straight at him then. So this was the other matter that he had wanted to talk about, she thought. It was only fair, she supposed, that the ex-wife be the first to know, before his plans were announced publicly.

He hadn't said that he was going to marry Tasha, she argued with herself. But that must be what he meant. In any case, it can't matter to me.

'I'm sure she'd appreciate being able to make some of those decisions,' she agreed tightly. 'I understand Katie has a room here.'

'The old nursery, at the top of the stairs. I hope you don't mind, Stephanie.'

'She'll need a place to take a nap sometimes, I'm sure. May I see it?'

He gestured towards the tower stairs.

Katie's bedroom was like a wonderland. The carpet was so thick and plush that bare toes could never be cold. On the walls were painted cartoon characters, each one painstakingly perfect, exactly as they appeared in her room at home.

'She wanted it to be as much like her other room as possible,' Jordan said. 'We compromised on the carpet.'

Stephanie had to smile. It sounded so very much like Katie, she thought, and remembered the day when Katie had refused the possibility of a new room at the

Anderson house. 'There's no bed,' she observed.

'Not yet. I can't find one that she approves of.'

'Perhaps she just said that because she doesn't want to take naps.'

'I hadn't thought of that. She says she wants a bed just like her other one, with the dolls' house headboard.'

'That will be difficult, since my father built it for her,' Stephanie pointed out.

'I was afraid it would be something like that. I'll keep trying.'

'It's thoughtful of you to go to so much trouble to make her feel at home, Jordan.'

His jaw tightened. 'It isn't thoughtful, Stephanie,' he said roughly. 'It isn't one damn bit thoughtful. I want this to be her home!'

Stephanie sucked in a frightened breath. It had finally come. She gathered all her strength, and said quietly, 'I know I was wrong not to tell you about her. And I understand that you'd like to have a bigger part in her life. Perhaps she could stay here on weekends or special times. And—'

'That's not enough, Stephanie.'

She looked at him, levelly. 'It will have to be enough. Because anything else is out of the question. It just isn't possible.'

'But you see,' he said softly, 'I think it is possible. Shall we look at the rest of the house now?'

She was a little shaky as she turned towards the master bedroom, both from that brief clash of words and from fear of what she might see in his room. But surely he wouldn't invite her there if Tasha's things were scattered about. Even if the woman was sleeping there, surely he wouldn't throw that evidence in Stephanie's face . . .

The room was painstakingly neat. There was a little more personality here; she thought he must be using it as a retreat and a living room until the ground floor was done. Two blue velvet chairs were placed by one window, a lamp table between them. Before the fireplace, where a dying fire flickered behind the glass screen, lay an enormous white fur rug . . .

The memory of words spoken long ago echoed in her ears. 'Lying on a rug in front of a blazing fire, making love on a cold night,' he had said.

It isn't fair, she thought. I shouldn't have to see this, and know that it will be Tasha who sleeps here with him . . . I have to get out of here, she thought.

She turned towards the door, haste making her clumsy, and only then did she really see the bed. The brass headboard was almost ceiling high, with intricate scrollings forming a complicated pattern. The footboard was nearly as elaborate.

I've seen that bed before, she thought. It was in the attic, covered with paint . . .

Tears brimmed in her eyes. Damn it, she thought, it belongs to him, he can do with it what he wants. But why did he bring me in here? To show it off? To please me by showing me that he followed my suggestions?

'It's lovely,' she said, and tried to be discreet as she brushed a hand over her eyes.

But he saw. 'Stephanie—don't cry. Please don't cry.' He put a gentle arm around her, and kissed a tear away.

'Then don't hurt me,' she said, her voice breaking. 'Don't be nasty to me.'

'I can't seem to help it.'

She started to sob, and clung to him. He held her till the worst had passed.

'I'm sorry,' she muttered. 'I don't know what's the matter with me . . .'

There was a brief silence, then he said, 'Steph, is there any chance—'

She said, with a sudden flash of anger, 'That I'll let you take Katie from me? Never!'

He looked down at her for a long moment, with brooding intensity. Then he kissed her, with harsh urgency, and again, more gently. She started to protest, but he would not let her go, and her words came out jumbled against his demanding mouth. 'Hush,' he ordered. His fingers had tangled into her hair, and he was holding her so that she could not pull free.

Abruptly, she stopped fighting. The power of that mesmerising kiss had left her stunned and helpless, wanting only to be there in his arms, to be part of him, to never have to leave him. The ache inside her that she had tried to forget in the long years they had been apart was harsher now. It was a bitter scar, this hurt they had caused each other, and she longed to hold him close and try to heal the pain in the only way they had ever known.

'Stephanie,' he breathed, and held her closer. There was no element of force left as his hands wandered through her hair, down over her shoulders, to cup her hipbones and pull her so close that the warmth of his body seemed to seer her skin.

I don't care, she thought. I don't care what tomorrow brings, as long as I can have him tonight. She reached blindly for the buttons on his shirt, and her fingers trembled as she unfastened them.

He groaned, and suddenly he picked her up and put her on the bed. The hunger between them was so deep that there could be no words for it. Only their bodies could express this longing.

The last button on his shirt yielded, and he shrugged out of it. 'My God,' she said, and her voice shook, 'I'd forgotten how beautiful you are . . .'

'Beautiful?' he asked, breathlessly.

She nodded, and then, only half-conscious of the words, said, 'Make love to me tonight, Jordan, and you can have whatever you want. I can't refuse you . . . I never could . . .'

For a moment he was still, his lips still pressed against her breast where the lacy cup of her bra ended. Then, with an oath, he rolled away from her.

'Jordan?' she said.

He sat on the edge of the bed, his face in his hands. 'I can't do it, Stephanie,' he said. His voice was hoarse, rough. 'I brought you here tonight to seduce you. I planned it—I cold-bloodedly planned how to get you into my bed, and when you asked about the kitchen —But I can't go through with it.'

A little hammer seemed to be crashing away at the back of her head, and the shock waves reverberated through her brain.

Are you crazy, it seemed to be asking. Are you crazy? Are you CRAZY?

She wanted to scream curses at him. She wanted to fly at him and pound her fists against his chest. She wanted to run away and never, never see him again.

She buttoned her blouse with shaking fingers, tucked it in, and said, 'Will you take me home now?' Her voice was jerky, uneven.

He didn't seem to hear her. He just sat there on the edge of the bed and said, 'That's just it, you see, Stephanie. I could always win our arguments—in bed. It has to be different this time. We can't solve this problem in bed. And if we don't solve it, we don't have any hope of a future.'

'A future?' she said, uncertainly. 'For us? What kind of a joke is this?'

He looked up, his eyes dark and intense. 'I wasn't asking you to give up Katie. I want you both to come home. To Whiteoaks.'

It took a moment for her dazed brain to process what he had said, and then she looked up with astonishment in her eyes.

'You want me to live here? With you?'

'Yes,' he said, eagerly. 'Stephanie—'

For a moment, she lost herself in the dream of what it could be like. The two of them, together, with Katie—

And then she remembered that instant when she had

offered him everything in the world she had to give, and he had turned away, unable to make love to her, even with all his carefully made plans.

To be with him, without the physical love they had shared, would be impossible. 'No,' she said. 'I understand, Jordan, but—'

'You can't understand, dammit. In the years since you left me—'

It stung her pride. 'You're the one who left me, Jordan.'

'I was going to come back for you,' he said. 'To tell you that I wouldn't stand any more nonsense, that you'd married me and you were coming with me. Then the divorce papers came.'

'I thought that it was over, that we might as well end it.'

'I thought it was over, too,' he said. 'I tried to put you behind me, to pretend that you had never been. There have been other women. I won't deny that, I can't. But every time I was with one of them, I was thinking about you. You were always there, just off to the side, where I could never quite see you clearly. But you haunted me.'

Fair is fair, she thought, remembering the times she had kissed Tony, and thought of Jordan.

'Then I came here and saw you again. And you were almost the same woman I remembered. Almost. That was bad enough. I hoped, I think, that you'd have grown sharp and ugly, and all angles—'

I might have, she thought, if it hadn't been for Katie.

'I thought it was Tony who had made you softer and sweeter. I think I could have killed him then, believing that he had made you gentle, when I couldn't.' He paused, and then said, very deliberately, 'When I, who loved you so very much, only made you angry and hateful and spiteful.'

'I was afraid of you,' she said. 'That first night you were so angry—'

'You were standing there with Tony's arm around you,' he reminded. 'You insisted that you were going to marry him. It hurt to think that you had forgotten me so easily. Then I found out about Katie.'

'You don't have to do this, you know,' she said clearly. 'It won't change my mind. I will never give Katie up. I'll fight till I've spent my last dollar and my last tear, but I will not—'

'Do you think this is for Katie?' His voice was low and furious. 'If Katie was all I wanted, I'd have taken you a few minutes ago without a second thought, and enjoyed myself, too. Can't you see, damn it? It's you I want, Stephanie!'

'You kept telling me you didn't care what I did.' Stephanie's knees were shaking so badly that she wanted to sit down, but she was afraid she couldn't walk across the room to a chair.

'I was trying to convince myself, every time I said that. I pretended that you didn't matter any more. The day you were sick,' he said gently, 'your nose was red, and your voice was croaky, and you looked like hell, and you were still the most beautiful woman in the world.'

'You didn't contest the divorce,' she said. It sounded like someone else talking.

'Lawyers cost money, Stephanie. I was broke, living from hand to mouth, those first few months. By the time the money started to come, it was too late—there was nothing left to fight for. You hadn't even told me yourself that you were filing. Just those cold papers dropped on me by a sheriff's deputy.'

'But now there's Katie,' she said bitterly.

'I didn't know about Katie when I bought the McDonald plant.'

'It must have come as a horrible shock, to meet me in the country-club dining room!' She turned away, not wanting to see confirmation in his eyes.

'This town is a good location for my business, but so

were a half-dozen others. No, I didn't expect to see you at the club that night, but I did expect to look your parents up as soon as I got settled and ask them where you'd gone. Finding that you were actually living here was a bonus.'

'And Tasha?' Her voice was hoarse.

Jordan smiled and brushed a lock of hair back from her cheek. 'She's going back east after Christmas. Thank heaven.'

'You don't—love her?'

'How can I? There's this fiery little redhead in the way.' There was a smile in his voice, and then he sobered. 'You read something at our wedding. Remember it? "Entreat me not to leave thee",' he quoted softly, '"or to return from following after thee. Whither thou goest will I go . . ."'

She closed her eyes, and listened to the echo from the past.

'Did you mean it, when you said that? Or was it just words? I followed you, Stephanie. Not Katie, but you. Now it's up to you. Do we try again, or do we say goodbye?'

'Why now?' she said. 'Why not two weeks ago, when I gave Tony's ring back?'

'I wanted to have a home to bring you to, not a crumbling hulk. I wanted you to see what I can offer you now—'

She brushed a hand across her wet cheek and shook her head.

'But tonight, I couldn't be patient any longer. I had to know—Stephanie?'

She swallowed hard. Her throat was so tight that it hurt to talk. 'I waited for you to come back,' she whispered. 'I thought it was important that you say you were sorry. I wish I hadn't been so stubborn, and so selfish, and so proud . . .'

He didn't kiss her, then. They clung together as if they

were starving, not for sexual closeness, but for sheer human warmth.

'I want to try again, Jordan.' Her voice was husky, and he cupped her face in his hands as if afraid that he hadn't heard right.

We nearly froze to death because of our childish pride, she thought, humbly. And now that we've both grown up, we are given the rare gift of being able to start over. Older, wiser—past the dreadful mistakes of youth. I will never let go of this man again, she thought. No, that's wrong. I will let him be free, because now I can trust as well as love . . .

'I hate to mention it,' he said, finally, stroking her hair. 'But I'm only human, and if you don't intend to make love with me tonight, then you'd better take yourself off to another room. That's fair warning, Steph —and the only one you're going to get.'

'We aren't married, you know.'

He said firmly, 'The divorce is purely a technicality, easily remedied. As far as I'm concerned, Stephanie Kendall, you have always been my wife.'

The blinding light in his eyes took her breath away. It took a long time for her to find words and fit her tongue to them. 'It's late,' she sighed, regretfully. She didn't move her head from his shoulder. 'We'd better pick up Katie before Mom reports us missing.'

He rubbed his cheek against her hair and said blandly, 'Katie is staying overnight.' There was a smile in his voice.

'When did you arrange that?'

'When I called your mother.'

'You really did plan this, didn't you?' She pulled away from him just far enough to see his face. 'And she helped you.'

A faint smile played around his mouth. 'Let's say that your mother and I had a hypothetical discussion a couple of weeks ago.' He pulled her close again. 'Do you know—I've been wishing all day that Katie hadn't told me about you being in the shower when I called this morning. I keep thinking about you standing there dripping, wearing nothing but a towel, and it's played havoc with my peace of mind—'

'It would be a shame to waste all that planning,' Stephanie said softly. 'Wouldn't it?'

'Welcome home, darling,' he said, and then there was no more need for words.

Six exciting series for you every month... from Harlequin

Harlequin Romance
The series that started it all

Tender, captivating and heartwarming...
love stories that sweep you off to faraway places
and delight you with the magic of love.

♦

Harlequin Presents
Powerful contemporary love stories...as individual as the women who read them

The No. 1 romance series...
exciting love stories for you, the woman of today...
a rare blend of passion and dramatic realism.

♦

Harlequin Superromance®
It's more than romance...
it's Harlequin Superromance

A sophisticated, contemporary romance-fiction
series, providing you with a longer,
more involving read...a richer mix of complex plots,
realism and adventure.

Harlequin
American Romance™
Harlequin celebrates the American woman...

...by offering you romance stories written about American women, by American women for American women. This series offers you contemporary romances uniquely North American in flavor and appeal.

◆

Harlequin Temptation
Passionate stories for today's woman

An exciting series of sensual, mature stories of love...dilemmas, choices, resolutions... all contemporary issues dealt with in a true-to-life fashion by some of your favorite authors.

◆

Harlequin Intrigue
Because romance can be quite an adventure

Harlequin Intrigue, an innovative series that blends the romance you expect... with the unexpected. Each story has an added element of intrigue that provides a new twist to the Harlequin tradition of romance excellence.

Harlequin Books

ATTRACTIVE, SPACE SAVING BOOK RACK

Display your most prized novels on this handsome and sturdy book rack. The hand-rubbed walnut finish will blend into your library decor with quiet elegance, providing a practical organizer for your favorite hard-or soft-covered books.

Only $9.95

Approximately 16" x 8" when assembled

Assembles in seconds!

To order, rush your name, address and zip code, along with a check or money order for $10.70* ($9.95 plus 75¢ postage and handling) payable to *Harlequin Reader Service*:

Harlequin Reader Service
Book Rack Offer
901 Fuhrmann Blvd.
P.O. Box 1396
Buffalo, NY 14269-1396

Offer not available in Canada.

BKR-1A

*New York and Iowa residents add appropriate sales tax.